THE ENCHANTED WANDERER

The Enchanted Wanderer

A mystical discovery awaits

TINA MAREE

Tina Maree

CONTENTS

~ One ~

CHAPTER 1: THE FOOL'S AWAKENING

The fools journey

In the heart of a lush and vibrant landscape, bathed in the soft hues of dawn, the Fool awakens as if woven into existence by the cosmic threads of creation. The air carries a delicate fragrance of blooming flowers, and the leaves rustle in symphony with the awakening day. The radiant gaze of the sun, a celestial painter, bathes the scene in hues of gold and amber, casting long shadows that dance with the promise of adventure.

The Fool, a figure of whimsical allure, stands at the edge of a precipice, the chasm below cloaked in mysterious shadows. His attire is a tapestry of colours, each thread telling a story of distant lands and uncharted territories. A small knapsack, worn but filled with the weight of untold dreams, hangs over his shoulder. In his left hand, the white rose, a delicate emblem of purity, exudes an otherworldly glow, echoing the untainted potential that lies within.

With each step the Fool takes, the arcane landscape responds. The ground beneath him pulses with a subtle energy, an ancient heartbeat resonating with the rhythm of the cosmos. A loyal white dog, with fur as pristine as freshly fallen snow, moves gracefully by his side. Its eyes, reflective of cosmic mysteries, hold a silent pact to accompany the Fool through the unexplored realms.

The Fool's eyes, pools of innocence, gaze out into the horizon, oblivious to the abyss that awaits. He carries with him the essence of a divine spark, an ethereal fire that fuels the courage to embrace new beginnings. The landscape, a canvas of possibility, beckons him to the precipice, where the boundary between reality and the unknown blurs.

As the Fool steps into the uncharted territories, the air crackles with latent magic. The very essence of the universe seems to whisper secrets, promising revelations to the one who dares venture into the depths. A small bag of dreams swings at the Fool's side, a repository of aspirations awaiting manifestation in the cosmic dance of fate.

In this beginning chapter of the Fool's saga, the landscape unfolds like an intricate manuscript awaiting the quill's first stroke. The Fool, an unwitting protagonist, embraces the unfolding narrative with an open heart and an unquenchable thirst for the arcane. With each step, he inscribes the cosmic parchment with the ink of wonder and curiosity, his footprints like magic circling him becoming a testament to the dance between destiny and free will.

The echoes of potential resonate in every footfall, and the Fool, attuned to the mystical currents, dances forward into the mysteries that await—ready to script the first chapter of his magical odyssey. The air is pregnant with anticipation, and the vibrant landscape, with its myriad hues and textures, becomes the stage for the Fool's grand entrance into the tapestry of destiny.

So, as the Fool stands on the precipice of the unknown, with the vibrant landscape surrounding him, he feels a growing sense of anticipation and curiosity. Little does he know that his journey will soon lead him to a fateful encounter with the enigmatic Magician. And so, with the sun as his witness and the cosmos as his guide, his journey begins, leaving behind the footprints of a traveler destined for the extraordinary.

~ Two ~

CHAPTER 2: THE MAGICIAN'S RENDEZVOUS

Drawn to the spectacle like a moth to a flame, the Fool navigated through the bustling marketplace until he stood before the Magician, who had set his stage amidst the vibrant energy of life's activities.

In the mystical choreography of the landscape, the Fool's footsteps seemed to harmonise with the vibrations of some unseen forces. The magicians who stood before him, his eyes sparkled with the ancient wisdom of the cosmos, and a staff crackling with ethereal energy was held with a reverence that hinted at its arcane potency.

Adorned in elegant robes embellished with symbols of the four elements, the Magician became a magnetic presence. A sparkling goblet for water, a lit wand for fire, a sheathed dagger for air, and a pentacle for earth adorned his attire, each resonating with its own unique energy.

As the Magician gracefully gestured toward the elements on his table, manifestations transformed into tangible forms. Water flowed, fire danced, a gust of air swirled, and the pentacle remained steadfast. The Fool's eyes widened in astonishment at the spectacle of power and mastery before him.

Acknowledging the Fool's presence, the Magician greeted him with a voice that carried the weight of ancient secrets.

"Greetings, seeker of mysteries! What brings you to my humble stage?"

"Oh, great Magician, your spectacle has captured my soul! The dance of elements, the magic in the air—it's unlike anything I've ever seen. Who are you, and what secrets do you hold?"

"I am but a conduit for the cosmic energies, a weaver of the threads that connect the seen and the unseen. I am the Magician, and the secrets I hold are the keys to the vast tapestry of creation. But come closer, young one. What is your name, and what stirs within your heart that led you to this spectacle?"

"I am the Fool, a wanderer seeking the mysteries of existence. Your performance has ignited a fire within me, a hunger for understanding the hidden realms. Can you teach me, great Magician? Can you unlock the secrets that dance within the fabric of the cosmos?"

"Ah, the Fool! The seeker of the cosmic dance. You carry the spark of curiosity, and that, my friend, is the key to unlocking the mysteries. The elements dance to the rhythm of your questions. Watch closely."

With a flourish, the Magician continued his performance, guiding the Fool through the symbolic language of the elements.

"This is astounding! Can I, too, command the elements? Can I shape reality with the same mastery?"

"Indeed, Fool. As above, so below. The power to shape your destiny lies within. You are a co-creator in this cosmic dance. But remember, with great power comes great responsibility. Embrace your potential, and the universe shall respond."

The Magician's eyes met the Fool's, and a knowing smile played on his lips. It was as if he were silently inviting the Fool to explore the untapped depths of his own abilities, to reach into the source of his own creative power.

Symbols floated in the air, each carrying the weight of ancient alchemical secrets. With a graceful flourish, the Magician beckoned the Fool into the realm of manifestation. The elements responded to their command, converging in a breathtaking symphony that unfolded the secrets of conscious creation.

"I had no idea such power resided within me. How do I begin to understand and harness it, wise Magician?"

"The journey begins with self-awareness, Fool. Know thyself, trust your instincts, and embrace the creative force that courses through your veins. Take this wand, a symbol of your connection to the elements. Let it be a guide on your cosmic journey."

As the Magician handed the Fool the wand, a subtle current of energy passed between them—a transfer of wisdom and potential.

"Thank you, great Magician! I sense that this encounter is a turning point in my journey. What more awaits me on this mystical path?"

"The path unfolds with each step, Fool. Trust the dance of the cosmos within you, and you shall discover realms untold. Remember, the world is a stage, and you are the magician. Manifest your desires, shape your destiny, and let the cosmic dance guide your steps."

As the Fool walked away, the bustling marketplace faded into the background, and the echoes of the Magician's teachings lingered in his heart. The vibrant energy of the crowd became a symphony of possibilities, and the Fool, now aware of his own potential, continued his journey with a newfound sense of wonder and purpose. The stage was set, and the cosmic dance awaited his next steps.

~ Three ~

CHAPTER 3: THE HIGH PRIESTESS'S VEIL

After the Fool's encounter with the Magician, he continued his journey with a newfound sense of wonder and purpose. His path led him deeper into the forest, where the trees stood tall and ancient, their branches forming a natural cathedral overhead. The air was thick with a sense of reverence and mystery.

Enveloped in the magical afterglow of the Magician's teachings, the Fool continued his odyssey through the forest. As the cosmic currents guided him, the landscape transformed into a sacred grove adorned with moonlit blossoms.

As he ventured deeper into the woods, the atmosphere shifted. It became quieter, almost as if the very forest held its breath in anticipation of what lay ahead. The hush of the leaves and the soft rustling of animals created a serene backdrop for the next part of his journey.

Amidst the luminous blooms, the High Priestess materialised—a luminary cloaked in robes that mirrored the phases of the moon. Her eyes, ancient wellsprings of wisdom, beckoned the Fool into the depths of the unseen. The air resonated with an intuitive melody as the High Priestess extended a delicate invitation for the Fool to step beyond the veil.

And then, as if drawn by an invisible force, the Fool found himself standing before a stone dais, upon which the High Priestess sat. She was an embodiment of grace and enigma, her presence radiating an air of ancient knowledge.

Her dark, penetrating eyes were veiled by shadows, and her lips curled into a serene smile as she acknowledged the Fool's arrival. She was a figure of immense significance, a guardian of the hidden truths and the mysteries of the soul.

The High Priestess extended her hand, inviting the Fool to approach. He did so with a mixture of reverence and intrigue, aware that he stood in the presence of a being who held the keys to the deepest recesses of knowledge.

She spoke in a voice that was like a gentle, melodic whisper of the wind. Her words seemed to echo with the wisdom of ages long past.

"Welcome, young man and your faithful companion" the high priestess eyes danced like magic as she bestowed a beaming smile upon the fools four legged companion . "I am the guardian of veils, the keeper of the moonlit mysteries. What brings you to this sacred grove?"

"Great High Priestess, I come with an open heart, hungry for the wisdom that transcends the known. The Magician guided me through the dance of creation, and now I seek to understand the hidden realms of intuition."

"Ah, the dance of creation. The Magician, a master of cosmic manipulation, sets the stage for your journey. But now, we step into the subtle currents where intuition reigns supreme. Follow me, and let the moonlight reveal the secrets woven into the threads of your destiny" beckoned the High Priestess.

As the High Priestess guided the Fool deeper into the moonlit grove, symbols seemed to shimmer in the air, painting an ethereal tableau of esoteric truths.

Fool was In awe "What lies beyond the veil, Great High Priestess? What secrets does the moonlight hold for a seeker like me?"

"The dance continues, seeker. Beyond this moonlit grove, the tapestry of your destiny unfurls. Embrace the whispers, trust the symbols, and you shall navigate the unseen with the grace of one who understands the mystical language of the heart."

In the liminal space, where the seen and unseen converged, the High Priestess became a celestial guide—a conduit to the vast realms of inner knowing. Symbols and arcane glyphs danced in the moonlit air, weaving a silent narrative that spoke of cosmic truths hidden beneath the surface of consciousness.

With a knowing nod, the High Priestess conveyed the significance of intuition—a language beyond the confines of logic. The Fool, immersed in the mystique, felt the gentle whispers of the cosmos encouraging them to trust the silent currents that flowed from the depths of one's soul.

In the mystical embrace of the High Priestess, the Fool's senses tingled with anticipation. A sacred scroll, ethereal and weightless, materialised in the Fool's hands. As he unfurled the scroll, symbols illuminated with the ancient wisdom of ages, revealing the cryptic messages encoded in the very fabric of the cosmic dance.

The High Priestess, her gaze penetrating the veils of illusion, guided the Fool to recognise the significance of dreams and intuitions as celestial guides on their journey. The Fool, now a seeker of hidden truths, felt the resonance of the unseen weaving into the very fabric of their existence.

This enchanted chapter unfolded like petals unfurling in the moonlit grove. The Fool, enriched by the teachings of the High Priestess, emerged with a veiled awareness—an intuitive understanding that transcended the boundaries of ordinary perception.

The cosmic energies echoed with ancient whispers, and the Fool, now attuned to the subtle harmonies of the cosmic symphony, danced onward into the moonlit corridors of their mystical quest, a seeker in pursuit of the mysteries that awaited beyond the veils of perception.

The High Priestess showed the Fool how to trust his inner wisdom, to listen to the whispers of his intuition, and to pay attention to the dreams and visions that danced on the edges of his consciousness. She taught him that the answers to life's most profound questions often lay hidden within, waiting to be uncovered.

The Fool felt a profound sense of resonance with the High Priestess's teachings. It was as if she had opened a door to a realm of hidden knowledge, a place where the boundaries between the conscious and the subconscious blurred.

The encounter with the High Priestess left the Fool with a deep sense of inner calm and a profound awareness of the inner dimensions of his being. He realised that his journey was not just a physical adventure, but a quest for self-discovery and spiritual growth.

As he continued on his path, the Fool carried with him the High Priestess's teachings, knowing that the true treasures of his adventure lay not just in the external landscapes he would encounter but also in the uncharted territories of his own inner world.

The High Priestess had become his guide to the hidden realms of the soul, and he understood that this journey was as much about exploring the mysteries within as it was about discovering the mysteries of the external world.

~ Four ~

CHAPTER 4: THE EMPRESS'S EMBRACE

Guided by the wisdom of the High Priestess, the Fool's journey through the lush and mystical forest continued. The path led him deeper into the heart of nature, where the very air seemed to hum with life and vitality. Tall, ancient trees surrounded him, their branches forming a magnificent canopy overhead, dappled with the golden light of the sun.

As the fool and his dog walked along the winding trail, the forest became more vibrant, teeming with colourful blossoms, exotic plants, and creatures of all shapes and sizes. The scent of blooming flowers and the gentle hum of bees filled the air, creating a sense of natural abundance and fertility.

Then, as if emerging from the very essence of the forest itself, the Fool found himself in a serene, sunlit garden. In the heart of this garden, the Empress reigned, her presence nothing short of awe-inspiring.

"Welcome, my dear Fool how lovely to see you, In this enchanted garden, where every bloom and creature tells a tale of life's abundance. Come, sit beside me, and let the magic of creation unfold," she beckoned.

The Fool sat, and the Empress continued to share her wisdom. She spoke of the interconnectedness of all living things and the dance of the seasons, where nature's cycles mirrored those within the human soul.

"See how the river flows, nourishing the soil and bringing life to the garden. It is a reflection of the endless flow of creativity and abundance within you. Embrace the ebb and flow, for in harmony with these cycles, you shall discover the true richness of existence."

Encouraging the Fool to embrace his own creative energy, she spoke of nurturing ideas and dreams with the same care and love she bestowed upon her garden. Life's true richness, she revealed, came from tending to the seeds of potential within.

"Feel the heartbeat of the earth, dear Fool. It resonates with the pulse of creation. Every seed, every bloom, and every creature contributes to the grand tapestry of existence. Embrace the dance of life, and you shall find your place in the cosmic symphony."

The encounter left the Fool with a deep appreciation for the beauty and abundance of the world around him. As he continued his journey, he carried with him the Empress's teachings, knowing that the true treasures of his adventure lay not just in external landscapes but also in the fertile soil of his own creative spirit.

In the days that followed, the Fool continued through the enchanted forest it was here he felt the need to spend more time. The sunlit garden transformed into twilight, where trees whispered ancient secrets and mystical creatures stirred in the shadows.

Venturing deeper, the air became charged with otherworldly energy. Ethereal lights danced among the branches, casting a soft glow on the moss-covered ground. The forest seemed to come alive with the magic that pulsed through its veins.

In the heart of this enchanted twilight, the Fool discovered a secluded glade. Moonlight bathed the clearing, revealing a figure seated on a mossy throne—the Empress oh here the Empress was more beautiful if this was even possible. Her presence radiated a serene power, and the air was infused with the subtle fragrance of blooming flowers.

"Welcome again, My dear fool. In this realm of twilight, where shadows and light intertwine, you seek further wisdom. What stirs your heart, dear Fool?" the Empress inquired.

"Great Empress, your radiant garden left an indelible impression on my soul. Now, as I journey through the twilight, I yearn to understand the deeper mysteries that connect the realms of creation and growth. Can you unveil more of the cosmic tapestry for me?" the Fool asked.

Inviting him to sit on a carpet of soft moss, the Empress said, "Feel the heartbeat of the forest, the rhythm of creation that echoes through the ages. Here, amidst the dance of shadows and moonlight, let the secrets of the cosmos reveal themselves."

As the Fool sat, the Empress began to weave a lyrical narrative, each word a gentle stroke on the canvas of the universe. She spoke of the interconnectedness of all living things, the dance of the elements, and the sacred bond between the earthly and the divine.

"Look around, dear Fool. See how the moonlight caresses the leaves, and how the shadows create a canvas for the stars. It is in this delicate balance that creation finds its truest expression. The dance is not just about growth and abundance; it is about the cosmic harmony that permeates every corner of existence," she explained.

Entranced, the Fool observed the play of light and shadow in the glade. The very air seemed to shimmer with the mystical energy of her teachings.

"Empress, how can I attune myself to this cosmic harmony? How do I become a participant in the dance of shadows and light?" the Fool asked.

"Open your heart, dear Fool. Feel the pulse of the universe within. The dance is not a solitary endeavour; it is a symphony where each note contributes to the cosmic melody. Align your intentions with the natural rhythms, and you shall find yourself in harmony with the grand tapestry of creation," the Empress replied.

In this twilight realm, where the Empress's garden merged seamlessly with the dance of shadows, the Fool felt the threads of creation and cosmic harmony weaving together, guiding him further into the mystic embrace of the enchanted forest.

~ Five ~

CHAPTER 5: THE MYSTICAL REALM OF THE EMPEROR

The Fool's meandering journey through the bewitched forest unveiled a dimension suffused with ethereal grandeur. The once-vivid hues of the sunlit glade and the enchanting twilight gradually gave way to a richer tapestry of profound reds and resplendent golds. In the heart of this majestic realm, the Fool came face to face with the Emperor, seated atop a throne hewn from time-worn stone, his presence radiating a commanding aura that demanded both attention and respect.

"Hail, traveler. Within my dominion, order and structure hold sway. What compels you to tread the path to the Emperor's realm?" the ruler declared, his voice resonating like the distant rumble of thunder.

With a respectful bow, the Fool approached. "Great Emperor, I am drawn to fathom the very foundations that uphold the cosmic order. The Empress spoke of harmony, and now I yearn to un-ravel the intricate structure that supports this grand tapestry of existence."

The Emperor gestured for the Fool to draw near, symbols of authority and power adorning the throne—discipline, organisation, and the establishment of boundaries. "In the cosmic ballet, every element finds its appointed place. Just as the stars adhere to a celestial order, so too must the dance of life abide by the laws of structure. What queries weigh upon your heart, seeker?"

"Great Emperor, I seek to grasp the delicate threads of responsibility and authority. How does one wield power with discernment, ensuring that order serves the greater harmony?" the Fool inquired, his gaze fixed on the sovereign.

The Emperor expounded on the importance of erecting boundaries and fortifying a solid foundation. Authority, he explained, transcends mere control; it embodies stewardship. "As a benevolent ruler, govern your realm with impartiality and integrity. The cosmic dance flourishes when each participant comprehends their role and pays homage to the roles of others."

"How does one strike a harmonious balance between the rigidity of order and the fluidity of flexibility? Can spontaneity coexist within the structured dance of existence?" the Fool pondered, seeking deeper insights.

"Indeed, Fool. Structure provides a framework, yet within its confines, creative expression can unfold. A sagacious sovereign discerns when to adapt and when to stand unwavering. Flexibility within boundaries ensures resilience amidst the ever-changing rhythms of the cosmic dance," the Emperor elucidated, his words carrying the weight of ancient wisdom.

As the conversation unfolded, the Emperor delved into the intricacies of leadership, emphasising the need for clarity, discipline, and an unwavering commitment to the greater good. The Fool listened intently, absorbing the profound wisdom woven into the Emperor's decree.

"Remember, Fool, authentic authority arises not from the hunger for control but from a profound understanding of the interconnected web of existence. Embrace the responsibilities that accompany wielding power, and let your actions resonate with the harmonies of the cosmic dance," the Emperor concluded, his words echoing in the solemn space.

With a nod of gratitude, the Fool rose from the ancient stone throne, the weight of the Emperor's teachings settling deep within his heart. The somber yet enlightening energy of the Emperor's realm had left an indelible mark on his understanding of structure and authority within the vast tapestry of existence.

Continuing his journey through the enchanted forest, the Fool carried with him the profound lessons of the Emperor, mindful that the delicate equilibrium between order and spontaneity was a crucial facet of navigating the cosmic dance. The authoritative resonance of the Emperor's decree echoed in his every step as he ventured into the uncharted territories that awaited in the chapters yet to unfold.

The forest embraced the Fool as he moved deeper into its enchanting embrace. The foliage whispered ancient secrets, and the air hummed with the mystic energies of the realm. Each footfall seemed to resonate with the wisdom imparted by the Emperor, and the Fool felt a profound sense of purpose guiding his steps.

The path meandered through groves adorned with luminescent flora, casting an otherworldly glow upon the surroundings. Shadows danced in silent celebration, acknowledging the presence of one who had communed with the Emperor himself. The very essence of the forest seemed to weave a narrative, echoing the cosmic dance the Fool sought to understand.

As the Fool journeyed, he encountered mystical creatures whose eyes gleamed with ancient knowledge. They spoke in riddles, unraveling the secrets of the universe with cryptic phrases that resonated with the wisdom of ages. Each encounter added layers to the tapestry of the Fool's understanding, deepening his connection to the intricate dance of existence.

The forest, with its towering trees and winding paths, became a living testament to the cosmic order described by the Emperor. The Fool marvelled at the interconnectedness of all things, from the smallest dewdrop on a leaf to the grandeur of the celestial bodies above. The symphony of life echoed in every rustle of leaves and every creature's song, a harmonious composition that unfolded with each step.

In the heart of the forest, the Fool stumbled upon a serene glade bathed in the soft glow of moonlight. A tranquil pool reflected the star-studded sky above, and the air was imbued with an ethereal stillness. It was here that the Fool realised the profound truth the Emperor had hinted at—the cosmic dance was not just a concept but a living, breathing reality.

Seated by the edge of the pool, the Fool contemplated the reflections dancing on the water's surface. The Emperor's teachings echoed in his mind, and he understood that true mastery of the cosmic dance required not only intellectual understanding but a profound attunement to the rhythm of the universe.

As the Fool lingered in the tranquil glade, he became aware of a subtle yet powerful energy emanating from the very heart of the forest. It beckoned him, and with a newfound sense of purpose, he followed the pulsating currents of mystic force. Each step resonated with the lessons learned from the Emperor, and the forest itself seemed to guide him toward a revelation that awaited in the depth of its mystical core.

The journey continued, and the Fool descended into a realm where the boundaries between the material and the metaphysical blurred. The air shimmered with unseen forces, and the very fabric of reality seemed to undulate like a cosmic tapestry in constant flux.

In this surreal domain, the Fool encountered visions that transcended the limits of ordinary perception. Whispers of ancient prophecies, glimpses of cosmic events, and echoes of beings from realms beyond intertwined in a kaleidoscopic symphony. The Fool navigated this ethereal landscape with a sense of wonder and trepidation, for he was now on the threshold of profound revelations.

The mystical energies guided the Fool to a sacred nexus, a place where the threads of destiny converged. Here, he stood at the intersection of cosmic forces, witnessing the ebb and flow of existence in its most intricate patterns. It was as if time itself unfolded before him, revealing the interconnected destinies woven into the vast tapestry of the universe.

In this transcendent moment, the Fool felt a surge of enlightenment. The cosmic dance, with its order and spontaneity, structure and flexibility, was not merely a series of principles but a living, breathing expression of the divine. He understood that every being, every event, and every choice played a unique part.

With this knowledge and reflection The fool was ready to step further into his journey and so he descended....

~ Six ~

CHAPTER 6: THE ENCHANTED DISCOURSE WITH THE HIEROPHANT

Emerging from the ethereal depths of the enchanted forest, the Fool found himself in a moonlit clearing, surrounded by the whispers of ancient trees. At the heart of this sacred space stood an ancient oak, beneath which the Hierophant, draped in robes woven from the threads of starlight, awaited.

The moonbeams played upon the Hierophant's countenance, casting an otherworldly glow as the Fool approached with a heart open to the mystical. The sacred grove seemed to hold its breath, anticipating the profound exchange that was about to unfold.

"Welcome young travellers. The ancient spirits of the forest have foretold of your journey and the luminescence you carry. What brings you to the sanctum of the Hierophant?" the wise figure inquired, his voice a melodic harmony that resonated with the very essence of the moonlit grove.

The Fool, his senses heightened by the magical energies swirling around, bowed in reverence. "Great Hierophant, I come seeking further understanding on the path of the cosmic dance. The Emperor spoke of order and structure, and now I wish to delve into the enchantment that weaves the spiritual realms into the fabric of existence."

The Hierophant, eyes sparkling like ancient constellations, nodded in acknowledgment. "In this sacred grove, where the mystical energies converge, we unravel the threads of magic that underlie the dance of the cosmos. Speak, seeker, and let your words weave the enchantment that stirs within your soul."

Embraced by the enchantment of the grove, the Fool spoke of his quest for magical insight. "Great Hierophant, I seek to understand the connection between the seen and the unseen, the material and the metaphysical. How does one attune oneself to the unseen forces that shape the cosmic tapestry?"

The Hierophant, his gaze fixed on the moonlit canopy above, began to reveal the secrets of magical attunement. "To commune with the metaphysical, one must dance with the inner stillness. The rustle of leaves, the dance of shadows—all are spells whispered by the divine. Seek silence within, and you shall find the resonance with the sacred frequencies that echo through the cosmos."

The Fool, feeling the magical currents flowing through his being, posed another question, "Great Hierophant, in the cosmic dance, how does one discern the magical from the mundane? What guides the seeker in navigating the mystical realms?"

The Hierophant spoke of the art of discernment, emphasising the importance of intuition and magical guidance. "The magical reveals itself to those whose hearts are attuned to its melody. Trust your inner enchantment, for it is the wand of the mage within you. Seek wisdom from ancient grimoires, connect with the energies of sacred symbols, and let the whispers of the unseen be your guide."

As the moon continued its celestial dance, the conversation between the Fool and the Hierophant deepened. The Fool, eager to grasp the mysteries of magical illumination, inquired about the trials one might encounter on the path of higher enchantment.

"Great Hierophant, as one ventures deeper into the mystical realms, what magical trials may test the seeker's resilience? How does one navigate the shadows that may emerge on the path to enchanted enlightenment?" the Fool asked, his eyes reflecting a genuine thirst for magical wisdom.

The Hierophant, a sorcerer in the moonlight, spoke of the magical shadows that often accompany spiritual ascent. "The journey to magical enlightenment is not without its trials. The shadows are reflections of the inner realms, manifestations of unresolved enchantments seeking integration. Embrace the darkness, for within it lies the potential for profound transformation. As you confront the shadows, remember that the light of awareness banishes the deepest magical shadows."

The Fool, wrapped in the magical teachings of the Hierophant, continued to engage with the wise figure beneath the ancient oak. The conversation wove through topics of spell craft, sacred symbols, and the significance of community on the magical journey. Each exchange deepened the Fool's understanding of the interconnected threads that wove together the cosmic dance of existence.

In the enchanted hush of the sacred grove, the Hierophant shared insights into the mystical secrets of the soul, imparting teachings that transcended the boundaries of earthly time and space. The Fool, grateful for the guidance, felt a sense of magical expansion, as if the very air shimmered with the energy of higher realms.

As the conversation approached its magical climax, the Hierophant spoke of the Fool's destiny as a custodian of magical knowledge. "Seeker, you carry the enchantment of the Emperor and the insights of this sacred grove. As you continue your journey, remember that magical knowledge is a sacred spell. Share it with those who seek the light, for in the act of sharing, the cosmic dance finds resonance in the hearts of kindred spirits."

With a final incantation of blessing, the Hierophant bestowed a magical boon upon the Fool, who left the sacred grove with a heart brimming with newfound magical wisdom. The moonlit path unfolded before him, and the echoes of the Hierophant's magical teachings lingered like a spellbinding melody, guiding the Fool toward the next enchanted chapter in the cosmic dance of his existence.

As the Fool stepped away from the moonlit grove, a newfound luminescence enveloped him, resonating with the enchantments bestowed by the Hierophant. The forest, alive with mystical energies, seemed to shimmer in acknowledgment of the magical exchange that had taken place.

Guided by the whispers of the ancient trees, the Fool continued along the moonlit path, each step echoing with the rhythm of the cosmic dance. Yet, before he could transition to the next realm, a radiant figure, cloaked in an iridescent aura, appeared before him—an ethereal being, a guardian of the mystical realms.

"Hail, seeker of the enchanted tapestry. The Hierophant's blessings linger upon you. Before you venture forth, allow me to unveil a glimpse of the magical realms that await," the ethereal figure spoke, their voice a harmonious blend of celestial melodies.

With a wave of their hand, the forest transformed. The moonbeams refracted through the leaves, creating a cascade of iridescent sparkles that hung in the air like suspended stars. The very air hummed with the resonance of unseen enchantments, and the trees leaned in to share ancient secrets with the Fool.

"Behold, seeker, the Veil of Realms—a mystical tapestry interwoven with the threads of the magical cosmos. Each realm is a chapter, a vibrant thread in the cosmic dance. As you journey, the Veil will unveil realms of wisdom, challenge, and wonder. Trust the magic that guides you, and let your heart be your compass," the ethereal guardian intoned, their words reverberating with the power of hidden realms.

The Fool, enraptured by the kaleidoscopic display, felt a deep sense of connection to the unseen realms. He marvelled at the shifting tapestry, each realm a canvas of possibilities waiting to be explored. The guardian continued, "Within these realms, you shall encounter beings of magic, guardians of ancient knowledge, and challenges that will test the resilience of your enchanted spirit.

Embrace the magic woven into every thread, and remember that you are a weaver of destiny."

As the ethereal figure concluded their revelation, the forest returned to its serene state. The luminescence lingered, embedding the magical visions within the Fool's consciousness. Gratitude filled his heart, and he bowed to the ethereal guardian.

"Thank you, guardian of the Veil. I shall heed your guidance as I step into the realms that await. May the cosmic dance unfold with magic and wonder," the Fool expressed, a sense of purpose illuminating his eyes.

With a gentle smile, the ethereal guardian faded into the moonlit shadows, leaving the Fool with a charged sense of anticipation. As he resumed his journey, the moonlit path beckoned, and the Veil of Realms shimmered, revealing glimpses of the enchanting chapters yet to be unveiled.

With every step, the Fool embraced the magic within and the wisdom gained from the Hierophant's sanctum. The cosmic dance awaited its next participant, and the Fool ventured forth, ready to weave his destiny amidst the magical realms hidden behind the Veil. The moonlit grove faded into the distance, but the enchantments lingered, guiding the Fool toward the threshold of the next mystical realm in the grand tapestry of his extraordinary journey.

~ Seven ~

CHAPTER 7: THE LOVERS' EMBRACE

As the Fool traversed the moonlit archway, a warm dawn greeted him, painting the sky with hues of gold and rose. The air crackled with an energy that seemed to resonate with the beating of his own heart. Before him lay a realm adorned with blossoms of every conceivable hue, each petal seemingly infused with the essence of magic.

The Fool's senses were heightened as he stepped into this enchanting garden, a space where the scent of flowers hung sweetly and the air itself seemed to hum with an ethereal melody. At the heart of this floral symphony, he discovered the Lovers—two figures locked in an embrace, their energies swirling in a dance of union and duality.

An unspoken invitation lingered in the air as the Lovers turned their gaze toward the Fool. The cosmic energy enveloped him, and a sense of anticipation welled within his being. The garden seemed to respond to his presence, petals unfolding in a choreographed display of harmonious beauty.

"Hail, seeker of the cosmic tapestry. We are the Lovers, embodiments of union and duality," the figures spoke in unison, their voices weaving together like a celestial duet.

The Fool, standing amidst the vibrant blossoms, felt a mixture of awe and reverence. The energy of the Lovers enveloped him like a gentle breeze, and he bowed respectfully. "Great Lovers, I stand before you with a heart open to the wisdom you hold. The cosmic dance has led me here, and I seek to understand the essence of union and duality that you embody."

The Lovers smiled, their eyes reflecting the wisdom of countless journeys. "In our embrace, seeker, lies the dance of contrasts—the meeting of light and shadow, the union of opposites. We are the reflection of the cosmic truth that harmonises through diversity."

As the Fool engaged in conversation with the Lovers, he felt a sense of communion with the very heartbeat of the universe. The garden, alive with the magic of blossoms, mirrored the dance within his soul.

"Great Lovers, how does one navigate the dance of opposites in the cosmic tapestry? What wisdom guides the seeker in embracing the duality that exists within and around?" the Fool inquired, his gaze wandering between the contrasting hues of the blossoms.

The Lovers gestured toward the garden, where flowers of every shade stood side by side. "In the dance of opposites, seeker, lies the alchemy of existence. Embrace the contradictions within, for they are the threads that weave the rich tapestry of your being. Recognise the beauty in duality, for it is through contrast that the cosmic dance gains its depth and meaning."

The Fool, surrounded by the living metaphor of their words, observed the delicate balance between light and shadow in the garden. The Lovers continued, "As you journey, seek the balance between your inner opposites. Embrace the light and shadow within, for in their unity, you shall discover the true essence of the cosmic dance."

"Great Lovers, how does one discern true union in the cosmic dance of connections? What guides the seeker in forming bonds that resonate with the harmony of the universe?" the Fool questioned, his eyes reflecting a desire to understand the mysteries of genuine connection.

The Lovers spoke of the sacred nature of connections, emphasising the importance of authenticity and vulnerability. "True union arises when hearts resonate with the cosmic song. Seek connections that echo the rhythms of your soul, where authenticity intertwines with vulnerability. In the dance of hearts, let love be the guiding force that unites and transcends."

As the conversation unfolded, the Fool felt a profound connection to the energies of the Lovers. The garden, bathed in the soft glow of dawn, became a sanctuary where the dance of union and duality unfolded in every petal, in every breath of the enchanting breeze.

"Great Lovers, what challenges may arise in the seeker's quest for harmonious connections? How does one navigate the complexities of relationships on the path to cosmic unity?" the Fool inquired, aware of the nuanced dance relationships often entailed.

The Lovers acknowledged the challenges inherent in the dance of connections, their words resonating with a timeless understanding. "In the cosmic dance of connections, challenges are the tests that strengthen the bonds of the heart. Embrace the lessons that arise, and let compassion be your guide. For in navigating the complexities, you shall uncover the enduring beauty of authentic connections."

As the conversation with the Lovers continued, the Fool felt a deep resonance within, as if the secrets of profound connection were unlocking within his soul. The garden, bathed in the soft glow of dawn, became a sacred space where the dance of the Lovers mirrored the intricate steps of the cosmic tapestry.

With a sense of gratitude, the Fool expressed his appreciation, "Great Lovers, your wisdom has illuminated the path of cosmic connection. I carry your teachings in my heart as I step into the next chapter of the grand dance. May the threads of union and duality guide my steps."

The Lovers, their eyes shimmering with an ageless understanding, nodded in unison. "May the cosmic dance unfold with the beauty of interconnected hearts. Go forth, seeker, and let the tapestry of connections weave its magic through your journey."

Leaving the garden of the Lovers, the Fool felt the lingering enchantment of their embrace. The dawn bathed him in a golden glow as he moved toward the next archway, where the cosmic tapestry awaited its next revelation. The echoes of the Lovers' wisdom danced in his heart, and the rhythmic steps of the grand dance beckoned him forward into the realms yet to be unveiled. In the wake of this encounter, the Fool carried the fragrance of the blossoms and the essence of the Lovers' wisdom, a magical resonance that would linger in his soul as he continued to dance through the realms of the cosmic tapestry.

~ Eight ~

CHAPTER 8: THE CHARIOT'S EMBRACE

The Fool, having traversed the realm of the Lovers, entered a space that shimmered with an iridescent glow. The air crackled with a magnetic energy, and the scent of blooming blossoms lingered, intertwining with the mystical ambiance. Before him, a celestial chariot adorned with ethereal symbols awaited, drawn by mythical creatures with wings of starlight.

As he approached, the Chariot itself seemed to pulse with a life force—an animate vessel of cosmic energy. Seated within was a figure, resplendent in attire woven from the threads of moonbeams, their eyes reflecting the mysteries of the night sky.

"Good day Fool. I am the Chariot, and my realm is one of swift enchantment and celestial motion," the figure greeted, their voice a melodic blend of the night wind and the twinkling of distant stars.

The Fool, captivated by the celestial spectacle, bowed in acknowledgment. "Great Chariot, I stand before you in awe. The cosmic dance has guided me to your realm, and I seek to understand the enchantments you weave within the grand tapestry."

The Chariot smiled, and the very air seemed to respond, carrying the fragrance of celestial blooms. "In my realm, fool, we embrace the magic of swift transitions and the romantic dance of cosmic energies. What questions stir within you as you step into the realm of the Chariot?"

Eager to unravel the secrets of this magical realm, the Fool spoke, "Great Chariot, I wish to comprehend the nature of swift transitions in the cosmic dance. How does one navigate the rapid currents of change and transition with grace and magical finesse?"

The Chariot spoke of the art of swift transitions, emphasising the importance of inner balance and alignment with the cosmic currents. "In the dance of swift transitions, find your centre, Fool. Let your inner compass guide you, and trust in the magical flow of the cosmic currents. Swift transitions are not obstacles but gateways to new realms of enchantment. Embrace the change, and let the Chariot of destiny carry you with grace."

Inspired by the Chariot's words, the Fool posed another question, "Great Chariot, how does one harness the magical energy of celestial motion in the cosmic dance? What wisdom guides the seeker in aligning with the rhythms of the stars and the ebb and flow of cosmic tides?"

The Chariot spoke of celestial alignment, encouraging the Fool to attune himself to the rhythmic dance of the cosmos. "In the realm of the Chariot, seek connection with the celestial realms. Tune into the music of the stars, and let their energy guide your movements. The cosmic dance is a harmonious symphony, and as you align with the celestial rhythms, you become a conductor of the magical energies that shape the tapestry of existence."

As the conversation unfolded, the Fool felt a magnetic resonance with the Chariot's teachings. The celestial chariot, adorned with symbols that seemed to come alive, became a vessel of enchantment. The Chariot continued, "Great seeker, in the cosmic dance, how does one navigate the intersections of destiny and free will? What guides the seeker in steering the chariot of their own fate?"

The Chariot spoke of destiny and free will as intertwined threads in the cosmic tapestry. "In the dance of destiny and free will, understand that you are both the weaver and the woven. Embrace the threads of destiny that weave through your journey, but also grasp the reins of free will. Steer your chariot with intention, and let the dance of destiny be a partner in your cosmic journey."

Feeling the celestial energy pulsating within him, the Fool delved deeper into the conversation. "Great Chariot, how does one invoke the magic of romantic connections in the cosmic dance? What wisdom guides the seeker in creating harmonious bonds that transcend time and space?"

The Chariot spoke of romantic connections as echoes of a timeless dance, where hearts resonate across the ages. "In the realm of romantic connections, seeker, recognise the dance of souls. Seek resonance that transcends the constraints of time and space. Let the magic of connection be a melody that harmonises with the cosmic symphony. Through the dance of hearts, create a love that echoes through the tapestry of existence."

As the moonlit conversation between the Fool and the Chariot unfolded, the realm seemed to swirl with an enchanting energy. The cosmic chariot, now luminous with the Fool's understanding, became a vessel of infinite possibilities.

"Great Chariot, what challenges may arise as one navigates the swift currents of the cosmic dance? How does the seeker overcome obstacles and ride the chariot of destiny with resilience and magical prowess?" the Fool inquired, aware of the complexities that often accompanied swift transitions.

The Chariot acknowledged the challenges inherent in the dance of swift transitions, speaking of the importance of resilience and trust. "As you ride the chariot of destiny, seeker, obstacles may emerge like shadows on the cosmic path. Embrace the challenges as opportunities for growth. Trust in the magic within, and let resilience be your companion. In overcoming obstacles, you affirm your mastery of the cosmic dance."

The Fool, infused with the celestial teachings of the Chariot, expressed his gratitude. "Great Chariot, your wisdom has illuminated my path with a celestial radiance. I carry the resonance of your teachings as I continue to dance through the realms of the cosmic tapestry. May the swift transitions be guided by the magic of the Chariot's embrace."

The Chariot, their eyes reflecting the starlit expanse, nodded in acknowledgment. "May the cosmic dance unfold with the magic of celestial motion. Go forth, seeker, and let the chariot of destiny carry you to realms yet unveiled."

As the Fool left the realm of the Chariot, he felt the celestial energy lingering in his every step. The enchanted blooms whispered secrets of swift transitions, and the fragrance of cosmic blossoms accompanied him toward the next archway. The rhythmic dance of the cosmic tapestry echoed in his heart, and the Chariot's enchanting teachings illuminated his path as he ventured into the uncharted territories that awaited in the chapters yet to unfold.

$\sim$ N i n e $\sim$

CHAPTER 9: THE ENCHANTING
STRENGTH

As the Fool ventured through the archway, he found himself in a realm bathed in a soft, golden glow. The air was filled with a tranquil energy, and the scent of exotic blooms lingered in the gentle breeze. Before him stood a magnificent creature, a majestic lion with a coat woven from the hues of sunset. Seated beside the lion was a figure, radiating an aura of quiet strength and inner calm.

"Hail, seeker of the cosmic dance. I am the embodiment of Strength, and in my realm, we weave the enchantment of inner fortitude and gentle power," the figure greeted, their voice a soothing blend of the lion's purr and the rustle of leaves in a serene forest.

The Fool, captivated by the serene beauty of the realm, bowed respectfully. "Great Strength, I stand before you in awe. The cosmic dance has led me to your realm, and I seek to understand the magical essence you embody within the grand tapestry."

Strength smiled, and the lion beside them emitted a regal, harmonious growl. "In my realm, seeker, we explore the subtle magic of inner fortitude—the quiet strength that resides within every beating heart. What questions burn within you as you step into the realm of Strength?"

Eager to uncover the secrets of this tranquil realm, the Fool spoke, "Great Strength, I wish to comprehend the nature of inner fortitude in the cosmic dance. How does one cultivate the gentle power that resides within, and how does this strength manifest in the weave of the grand tapestry?"

Strength spoke of the enchantment of inner fortitude, emphasising the importance of compassion and self-awareness. "In the dance of inner fortitude, seeker, find strength in compassion and embrace the power of vulnerability. The quiet strength that shapes the cosmic tapestry is not about force but about the gentle power that flows from a heart attuned to its own resilience. Cultivate self-awareness, and let your inner strength be a beacon that lights the path for others in the cosmic dance."

Inspired by the words of Strength, the Fool posed another question, "Great Strength, how does one harmonise the energies of the heart and mind in the cosmic dance? What wisdom guides the seeker in balancing the emotional currents with the clarity of thought?"

Strength spoke of the delicate balance between heart and mind, encouraging the Fool to seek harmony within. "In the realm of Strength, find the dance of balance within your being. Let the heart and mind intertwine like vines in an enchanted garden. Embrace the emotional currents with an open heart, and let the clarity of thought be the compass that guides your steps in the cosmic dance."

As the conversation unfolded, the Fool felt a serene energy enveloping him. The realm, with its golden glow and the lion as a silent guardian, became a sanctuary where the dance of inner fortitude revealed itself as a tapestry woven with threads of compassion and wisdom.

"Great Strength, how does one navigate the complexities of personal transformation in the cosmic dance? What guides the seeker in embracing the changes that shape the tapestry of existence?" the Fool inquired, aware of the transformative nature of the cosmic journey.

Strength spoke of personal transformation as a magical process, where the seeker must embrace the alchemy of change. "In the dance of personal transformation, seeker, recognise the magic within the cocoon of change. Embrace the metamorphosis, for within it lies the emergence of your true self. Trust in the cosmic currents that guide your transformation, and let the strength within be the anchor as you unfold your wings in the grand tapestry."

Feeling the tranquil strength emanating from the lion's presence, the Fool delved deeper into the conversation. "Great Strength, how does one invoke the magic of resilience in the cosmic dance? What wisdom guides the seeker in overcoming challenges and adversity with grace?"

Strength spoke of resilience as the quiet force that rises from within, encouraging the Fool to trust in his own capacity to endure. "In the cosmic dance, seeker, resilience is the magic that strengthens the threads of your journey. Embrace challenges as opportunities for growth, and let the quiet strength within be the foundation upon which you stand. With grace and fortitude, you shall navigate the ebb and flow of cosmic currents."

As the moonlit conversation between the Fool and Strength continued, the lion's presence seemed to resonate with a regal serenity. The golden realm, now aglow with the wisdom of inner strength, became a haven where the cosmic dance unfolded with gentle power.

"Great Strength, what role does compassion play in the cosmic dance of connections? How does one foster harmonious bonds through the magic of empathy and understanding?" the Fool inquired, sensing the profound connection between strength and compassion.

Strength spoke of compassion as the heart's melody in the dance of connections, urging the Fool to weave threads of empathy into the cosmic tapestry. "In the realm of connections, seeker, let compassion be the enchanting thread that binds hearts together. Foster understanding, and let empathy guide your interactions. Through the gentle power of compassion, you shall create bonds that resonate with the harmony of the cosmic dance."

Expressing his gratitude, the Fool said, "Great Strength, your wisdom has brought a sense of calm to my cosmic journey. I carry the tranquility of your teachings as I continue to dance through the realms of the grand tapestry. May the quiet strength within guide my steps."

Strength, their eyes reflecting the serene wisdom of ages, nodded in acknowledgment. "May the cosmic dance unfold with the magic of inner fortitude. Go forth, seeker, and let the strength within be a beacon of light on your journey through the realms yet to be unveiled."

Leaving the realm of Strength, the Fool felt a tranquil energy lingering in his every step. The golden blooms whispered tales of inner fortitude, and the fragrance of exotic blossoms accompanied him toward the next archway. The rhythmic dance of the cosmic tapestry echoed in his heart, and the serenity of Strength's enchanting teachings illuminated his path as he ventured into the uncharted territories that awaited in the chapters yet to unfold.

As we tread this cosmic path, my faithful white companion, do you feel the enchanted forest sparking your curiosity, too? The Emperor's realm instills a sense of structure – quite different from the whimsical dance of the Lovers, isn't it? Their embrace echoes with profound connections, much like our own bond. And what about the Chariot's celestial motion? It propels us forward, stirring a sense of momentum in our journey, doesn't it?

I see you there, my loyal friend, with your tranquil presence. Strength's realm, with its calm aura, seems to resonate with the peaceful energy you bring to our adventures. A mosaic of awe, reverence, inspiration, and yearning paints our emotional landscape as we traverse these cosmic realms.

Here we stand at the threshold of the next realm. Can you sense the anticipation, my dear companion? The unknown lies ahead, waiting to unfold like a tapestry woven with magical threads – much like the soft fur beneath my fingers as we journey on.

As we step forward together, I feel the transformative echoes of wisdom and enchantment in our hearts. We embrace the currents of change, guided by the harmonious resonance of the realms behind us. I expect new revelations and hidden wonders, ready to converse with the mysteries that await us. Our journey continues, and I am grateful to have your silent company, dear friend, as we engage in the cosmic dance, seeking the magic that will shape the extraordinary chapters of our shared adventure.

~ Ten ~

CHAPTER 10: THE WHISPERING HERMIT

As the Fool stepped through the archway, he found himself in a realm bathed in a soft, silver glow. The air was hushed, and the only sound that echoed was a gentle, mystical breeze. In the heart of this serene space, the Hermit stood, cloaked in robes that seemed to shimmer with the reflections of a thousand stars. At his side, the Fool's loyal white dog companion sat, its eyes reflecting the wisdom of many journeys.

"Hail, seeker of the cosmic dance. I am the Hermit, keeper of the silent realms and seeker of the hidden truths," the Hermit greeted, his voice a soft murmur that echoed like distant whispers.

The Fool, acknowledging the tranquil atmosphere, bowed respectfully. "Great Hermit, I come with a heart open to the mysteries you guard. The cosmic dance has led me to your realm, and I seek to understand the hidden truths that shape the grand tapestry."

The Hermit, his gaze carrying the weight of contemplation, nodded in acknowledgment. "In this realm, seeker, we explore the magic of solitude and the illumination that comes from within. What questions stir within your heart as you step into the realm of the Hermit?"

Eager to unravel the secrets of this quiet space, the Fool spoke, "Great Hermit, I wish to comprehend the nature of solitude in the cosmic dance. How does one find the magic within the silence, and what wisdom guides the seeker in the journey of self-discovery?"

The Hermit spoke of the enchantment of solitude, emphasising the importance of inner reflection and the whispers of the soul. "In the dance of solitude, seeker, listen to the quiet echoes within. Find the magic in the stillness, for it is within the silence that the cosmic truths reveal themselves. Seek the illumination that comes from self-discovery, and let the whispers of your soul guide your steps in the grand tapestry."

Inspired by the Hermit's words, the Fool posed another question, "Great Hermit, how does one attune themselves to the cosmic rhythms in the dance of introspection? What wisdom guides the seeker in harmonising with the unseen forces that shape the universe?"

The Hermit spoke of cosmic attunement, encouraging the Fool to become a listener to the mystical symphony that surrounded him. "In the realm of introspection, seeker, become attuned to the cosmic rhythms. Listen to the unseen forces that shape the dance of the universe. Harmonise with the energies that flow through you, and let your introspective journey be a melody that resonates with the cosmic symphony."

As the conversation unfolded, the Fool felt a serene energy enveloping him. The silver realm, with the Hermit as a guide and the white dog companion by his side, became a sanctuary where the dance of introspection revealed itself as a tapestry woven with threads of self-discovery.

"Great Hermit, how does one navigate the labyrinth of the mind in the cosmic dance? What guides the seeker in discerning the truths hidden within the intricate corridors of thought?" the Fool inquired, aware of the complexities that often accompanied introspection.

The Hermit acknowledged the labyrinthine nature of the mind, his words carrying the weight of introspective wisdom. "In the dance of the mind, seeker, navigate the labyrinth with patience and curiosity. Discern the truths hidden within the intricate corridors of thought. Let introspection be a lantern that illuminates the shadows, and trust in the wisdom that emerges from the silent depths of your being."

Feeling the tranquil presence of the Hermit and the loyal dog companion, the Fool delved deeper into the conversation. "Great Hermit, how does one invoke the magic of intuitive guidance in the cosmic dance? What wisdom guides the seeker in trusting the whispers of the heart and the instincts that arise from the depths of the soul?"

The Hermit spoke of intuitive guidance as a sacred gift, encouraging the Fool to trust the whispers of the heart and the silent nudges of the soul. "In the realm of intuitive guidance, seeker, trust the whispers of your heart and the instincts that arise from the depths of your soul. Let your inner compass be your guide, for in the dance of intuition, the cosmic truths are revealed with gentle certainty."

As the moonlit conversation between the Fool, the Hermit, and the white dog companion continued, the realm seemed to shimmer with a mystical energy. The cosmic dance, guided by introspection and intuitive whispers, unfolded in every thoughtful step.

"Great Hermit, what challenges may arise in the seeker's quest for self-discovery and cosmic truths? How does one navigate the shadows that may emerge during the introspective journey?" the Fool inquired, aware of the nuanced dance that self-discovery often entailed.

The Hermit acknowledged the challenges inherent in the quest for self-discovery, speaking of the importance of resilience and inner light. "In the cosmic dance of self-discovery, challenges are the shadows that test your inner light. Navigate the shadows with resilience, and let the illumination from within guide your way. Embrace the lessons that arise, and let the dance of introspection be a transformative journey toward cosmic truths."

As the conversation with the Hermit unfolded, the Fool felt a deep resonance within, as if the secrets of self-discovery were unlocking within his soul. The silver realm, bathed in the soft glow of cosmic wisdom, became a sacred space where the dance of introspection mirrored the intricate steps of the cosmic tapestry.

With a sense of gratitude, the Fool expressed his appreciation, "Great Hermit, your wisdom has brought a sense of stillness and understanding to my cosmic journey. I carry the tranquility of your teachings as I continue to dance through the realms of the grand tapestry. May the whispers of self-discovery guide my steps."

The Hermit, his eyes reflecting the starlit expanse, nodded in unison. "May the cosmic dance unfold with the magic of introspection. Go forth, seeker, and let the silent whispers of self-discovery illuminate your path through the realms yet to be unveiled."

Leaving the realm of the Hermit, the Fool felt the tranquil energy lingering in his every step. The silver echoes of introspection whispered secrets of self-discovery, and the fragrance of cosmic blossoms accompanied him toward the next archway. The rhythmic dance of the cosmic tapestry echoed in his heart, and the Hermit's enchanting teachings illuminated his path as he ventured into the uncharted territories that awaited in the chapters yet to unfold.

~ Eleven ~

CHAPTER 11: THE EVER-TURNING WHEEL

As the Fool crossed the threshold into the next realm, he found himself surrounded by a kaleidoscope of swirling colours and the ethereal hum of celestial energy. In the centre of this mesmerising space, a grand wheel spun, adorned with symbols that seemed to dance with a life of their own. The air crackled with an enchanting energy, and the Fool sensed the ever-turning rhythm of fate.

A figure, draped in garments that mirrored the constellations, emerged from the dance of cosmic energies. "Greetings, seeker of the cosmic dance. I am the Keeper of the Ever-Turning Wheel, where destinies intertwine and the dance of fate unfolds," the figure announced, their voice a melodious blend of cosmic harmonies.

The Fool, captivated by the celestial spectacle, bowed respectfully. "Great Keeper of the Ever-Turning Wheel, I come with a heart attuned to the cosmic rhythms. The dance has led me to your realm, and I seek to understand the mysteries woven within the grand tapestry."

The Keeper of the Ever-Turning Wheel extended a hand, gesturing towards the celestial wheel. "In this realm, seeker, we explore the magic of destiny's dance and the interplay of cosmic forces. What questions stir within your heart as you step into the dance of fate?"

Eager to unravel the secrets of this dynamic space, the Fool spoke, "Great Keeper, I wish to comprehend the nature of destiny in the cosmic dance. How does one navigate the twists and turns of fate, and what wisdom guides the seeker in understanding the ever-turning wheel of life?"

The Keeper spoke of destiny as a celestial dance, emphasising the interconnected threads that wove through the grand tapestry. "In the dance of destiny, seeker, recognise the threads that connect you to the cosmic wheel. Navigate the twists and turns with an open heart, for the ever-turning wheel is a reflection of the intricate dance of life. Embrace the flow of fate, and let your journey be a harmonious part of the cosmic symphony."

Inspired by the Keeper's words, the Fool posed another question, "Great Keeper, how does one attune themselves to the cosmic energies that guide the dance of fate? What wisdom guides the seeker in aligning with the ebb and flow of the ever-turning wheel?"

The Keeper spoke of cosmic attunement, encouraging the Fool to become a participant in the cosmic dance. "In the realm of the ever-turning wheel, seeker, attune yourself to the cosmic energies. Feel the ebb and flow of the wheel, and let your steps be in harmony with the cosmic currents. Align with the rhythm of life, and become a conscious partner in the dance of fate."

As the conversation unfolded, the Fool felt a dynamic energy enveloping him. The realm, with its swirling colours and the ever-turning wheel at its centre, became a vortex of fate where the dance unfolded with intricate precision.

"Great Keeper, how does one invoke the magic of personal agency in the cosmic dance? What wisdom guides the seeker in shaping their destiny amidst the forces of the ever-turning wheel?" the Fool inquired, aware of the balance between fate and personal choices.

The Keeper acknowledged the dance of agency within the cosmic tapestry, speaking of the power of conscious choices. "In the cosmic dance of personal agency, seeker, recognise the potency of your choices. Shape your destiny with intention, for the ever-turning wheel responds to the conscious dance of your actions. Embrace the magic of agency, and let your choices echo in the cosmic symphony."

Feeling the dynamic energies pulsating within him, the Fool delved deeper into the conversation. "Great Keeper, how does one navigate the cycles of fortune and misfortune in the cosmic dance? What wisdom guides the seeker in embracing the ever-turning wheel with equanimity and grace?"

The Keeper spoke of the cycles inherent in the dance of fate, encouraging the Fool to find balance in the midst of fortune and misfortune. "In the realm of cycles, seeker, navigate the ever-turning wheel with equanimity. Embrace the cycles of fortune and misfortune as integral parts of the cosmic dance. Find grace in both the ascent and descent of the wheel, and let your journey be a reflection of the eternal dance of life."

As the moonlit conversation between the Fool and the Keeper continued, the realm seemed to swirl with an enchanting energy. The ever-turning wheel, now a kaleidoscope of destiny's dance, became a vessel of infinite possibilities.

"Great Keeper, what challenges may arise as one embraces the dance of fate? How does the seeker overcome obstacles and ride the ever-turning wheel with resilience and magical prowess?" the Fool inquired, aware of the complexities that often accompanied the twists and turns of destiny.

The Keeper acknowledged the challenges inherent in the dance of fate, speaking of the importance of resilience and a deep connection to the cosmic energies. "As you ride the ever-turning wheel, seeker, challenges may emerge like eddies in the cosmic stream. Embrace the challenges as opportunities for growth. Connect with the cosmic energies, and let resilience be your companion. In overcoming obstacles, you affirm your mastery of the cosmic dance."

The Fool, infused with the cosmic teachings of the Keeper, expressed his gratitude. "Great Keeper, your wisdom has unveiled the mysteries of destiny's dance. I carry the resonance of your teach-ings as I continue to waltz through the realms of the grand tapestry. May the ever-turning wheel guide my steps."

The Keeper of the Ever-Turning Wheel, their eyes reflecting the cosmic symphony, nodded in acknowledgment. "May the cosmic dance unfold with the magic of destiny's rhythm. Go forth, seeker, and let the ever-turning wheel carry you to realms yet unveiled."

Leaving the realm of the Ever-Turning Wheel, the Fool felt the dynamic energy lingering in his every step. The swirling colours whispered tales of destiny's dance, and the fragrance of celestial blossoms accompanied him toward the next archway. The rhythmic dance of the cosmic tapestry echoed in his heart, and the Keeper's enchanting teachings illuminated his path as he ventured into the uncharted territories that awaited in the chapters yet to unfold.

~ Twelve ~

CHAPTER 12: THE ENCHANTED SCALES

As the Fool stepped into the next realm, he found himself surrounded by an atmosphere of profound balance. A river of iridescent light flowed gently, and at its centre, a pair of luminous scales hung suspended, exuding an ethereal glow. In the heart of this harmonious space, a figure adorned in robes of shifting hues approached, their presence radiating an aura of impartial wisdom.

"Greetings, seeker of the cosmic dance. I am the Guardian of the Enchanted Scales, where the harmonies of justice and equilibrium weave through the cosmic tapestry," the figure greeted, their voice a melodic blend of celestial notes.

The Fool, mesmerised by the celestial scales, bowed respectfully. "Great Guardian of the Enchanted Scales, I come with a heart open to the melodies of justice. The dance has led me to your realm, and I seek to understand the harmonies woven within the grand tapestry."

The Guardian of the Enchanted Scales extended a hand, gesturing towards the luminous scales. "In this realm, seeker, we explore the magic of justice and the equilibrium that balances the cosmic energies. What questions stir within your heart as you step into the dance of impartiality?"

Eager to unravel the secrets of this balanced space, the Fool spoke, "Great Guardian, I wish to comprehend the nature of justice in the cosmic dance. How does one navigate the complexities of fairness, and what wisdom guides the seeker in understanding the harmonies of the enchanted scales?"

The Guardian spoke of justice as a cosmic melody, emphasising the importance of fairness and the interplay of energies. "In the dance of justice, seeker, recognise the harmonies that echo through the cosmic tapestry. Navigate the complexities with an open heart, for the enchanted scales respond to the impartial dance of your actions. Embrace the magic of fairness, and let your journey be a harmonious part of the cosmic symphony."

Inspired by the Guardian's words, the Fool posed another question, "Great Guardian, how does one attune themselves to the cosmic energies of equilibrium? What wisdom guides the seeker in aligning with the balance that flows through the enchanted scales?"

The Guardian spoke of cosmic attunement, encouraging the Fool to become attuned to the energies of balance. "In the realm of equilibrium, seeker, attune yourself to the cosmic energies. Feel the balance that flows through the enchanted scales, and let your steps be in harmony with the cosmic currents. Align with the equilibrium of life, and become a conscious partner in the dance of impartiality."

As the conversation unfolded, the Fool felt a serene energy enveloping him. The realm, with its luminous scales and the Guardian as a guide, became a sanctuary where the dance of justice revealed itself as a tapestry woven with threads of impartiality.

"Great Guardian, how does one invoke the magic of integrity in the cosmic dance? What wisdom guides the seeker in maintaining a true and just heart amidst the intricacies of existence?" the Fool inquired, aware of the nuances that often accompanied the pursuit of justice.

The Guardian acknowledged the importance of integrity within the cosmic tapestry, speaking of the power of a just and true heart. "In the cosmic dance of integrity, seeker, recognise the potency of a true and just heart. Uphold the principles that resonate with fairness, for integrity is the beacon that guides your steps in the dance of justice. Embrace the magic of integrity, and let your actions echo in the cosmic symphony."

Feeling the balanced energies resonating within him, the Fool delved deeper into the conversation. "Great Guardian, how does one navigate the challenges of upholding justice in the cosmic dance? What wisdom guides the seeker in facing obstacles with grace and impartiality?"

The Guardian spoke of the challenges inherent in the pursuit of justice, encouraging the Fool to face obstacles with equanimity. "In the realm of challenges, seeker, navigate the dance of justice with grace. Embrace obstacles as opportunities for growth, and let your pursuit of fairness be unwavering. Face the complexities with impartiality, and let the enchanted scales be your guide through the cosmic symphony."

As the moonlit conversation between the Fool and the Guardian continued, the realm seemed to glow with an enchanting energy. The enchanted scales, now a river of luminous light, became a vessel of cosmic justice where the dance unfolded with exquisite precision.

"Great Guardian, what role does compassion play in the cosmic dance of justice? How does one foster fairness through the magic of empathy and understanding?" the Fool inquired, sensing the profound connection between justice and compassion.

The Guardian spoke of compassion as the heart's melody in the dance of justice, urging the Fool to weave threads of empathy into the cosmic tapestry. "In the realm of justice, let compassion be the enchanting thread that binds hearts together. Foster understanding, and let empathy guide your pursuit of fairness. Through the magic of compassion, you shall contribute to the harmonious dance of justice."

Expressing his gratitude, the Fool said, "Great Guardian, your wisdom has brought a sense of balance and understanding to my cosmic journey. I carry the serenity of your teachings as I continue to dance through the realms of the grand tapestry. May the enchanted scales guide my steps."

The Guardian of the Enchanted Scales, their eyes reflecting the luminous balance, nodded in acknowledgment. "May the cosmic dance unfold with the magic of justice. Go forth, seeker, and let the enchanted scales carry you to realms yet unveiled."

Leaving the realm of the Enchanted Scales, the Fool felt the balanced energy lingering in his every step. The river of luminous light whispered tales of justice's dance, and the fragrance of celestial blossoms accompanied him toward the next archway. The rhythmic dance of the cosmic tapestry echoed in his heart, and the Guardian's enchanting teachings illuminated his path as he ventured into the uncharted territories that awaited in the chapters yet to unfold.

$$\sim \text{Thirteen} \sim$$

CHAPTER 13: THE HANGED HARMONY

As the Fool entered the next realm, he found himself surrounded by an otherworldly stillness. The air was hushed, and a gentle mist hung in the space like a veil between worlds. In the centre, a figure suspended upside-down from a gnarled tree, their expression serene and contemplative. The energy of surrender and introspection permeated the realm.

"Greetings, seeker of the cosmic dance. I am the Keeper of the Hanged Harmony, where the magic of letting go and embracing the unknown weaves through the cosmic tapestry," the figure greeted, their voice a soft, soothing breeze that carried a sense of timeless wisdom.

The Fool, captivated by the serene atmosphere, bowed respectfully. "Great Keeper of the Hanged Harmony, I come with a heart open to the mysteries of surrender. The dance has led me to your realm, and I seek to understand the enchantments woven within the grand tapestry."

The Keeper of the Hanged Harmony acknowledged the Fool's presence with a tranquil nod. "In this realm, seeker, we explore the magic of surrender and the serenity that arises from embracing the unknown. What questions stir within your heart as you step into the dance of surrender?"

Eager to unravel the secrets of this serene space, the Fool spoke, "Great Keeper, I wish to comprehend the nature of surrender in the cosmic dance. How does one find peace in letting go, and what wisdom guides the seeker in understanding the enchantments of the Hanged Harmony?"

The Keeper spoke of surrender as a cosmic release, emphasising the transformative power of letting go. "In the dance of surrender, seeker, find peace in the release of attachments. Embrace the unknown, for the Hanged Harmony arises when you let go of the need to control. Trust in the cosmic currents, and let your journey be a serene surrender to the ebb and flow of the grand tapestry."

Inspired by the Keeper's words, the Fool posed another question, "Great Keeper, how does one attune themselves to the cosmic energies of surrender? What wisdom guides the seeker in aligning with the tranquility that flows through the Hanged Harmony?"

The Keeper spoke of cosmic attunement, encouraging the Fool to become attuned to the energies of letting go. "In the realm of surrender, seeker, attune yourself to the cosmic energies. Feel the tranquility that flows through the Hanged Harmony, and let your steps be in harmony with the cosmic currents of release. Align with the serenity of letting go, and become a conscious partner in the dance of surrender."

As the conversation unfolded, the Fool felt a serene energy enveloping him. The realm, with its suspended figure and the Keeper as a guide, became a sanctuary where the dance of surrender revealed itself as a tapestry woven with threads of peaceful release.

"Great Keeper, how does one invoke the magic of self-discovery in the cosmic dance of surrender? What wisdom guides the seeker in exploring the depths of their being while letting go of preconceived notions?" the Fool inquired, aware of the introspective journey that often accompanied surrender.

The Keeper acknowledged the intertwining dance of surrender and self-discovery, speaking of the importance of exploring one's inner depths. "In the cosmic dance of self-discovery, seeker, explore the depths of your being as you let go of preconceived notions. Embrace the magic of surrender, and let the unknown unveil the mysteries within. Trust in the process, and let the Hanged Harmony guide your steps through the cosmic symphony."

Feeling the tranquil energies resonating within him, the Fool delved deeper into the conversation. "Great Keeper, how does one navigate the challenges of surrender in the cosmic dance? What wisdom guides the seeker in facing the uncertainties with grace and tranquility?"

The Keeper spoke of the challenges inherent in the dance of surrender, encouraging the Fool to face uncertainties with an open heart. "In the realm of challenges, seeker, navigate the dance of surrender with grace. Embrace uncertainties as opportunities for growth, and let your surrender be a testament to your trust in the cosmic currents. Face the unknown with tranquility, and let the Hanged Harmony be your guide through the cosmic symphony."

As the moonlit conversation between the Fool and the Keeper continued, the realm seemed to glow with a tranquil energy. The suspended figure, now a symbol of surrender's grace, became a vessel of cosmic release where the dance unfolded with gentle precision.

"Great Keeper, what role does compassion play in the cosmic dance of surrender? How does one foster kindness towards oneself and others while embracing the magic of letting go?" the Fool inquired, sensing the profound connection between surrender and compassion.

The Keeper spoke of compassion as the heart's melody in the dance of surrender, urging the Fool to weave threads of kindness into the cosmic tapestry. "In the realm of surrender, let compassion be the enchanting thread that binds hearts together. Foster kindness towards yourself and others, and let the dance of surrender be a testament to the magic of compassion. Through the Hanged Harmony, you shall contribute to the harmonious dance of the cosmic symphony."

Expressing his gratitude, the Fool said, "Great Keeper, your wisdom has brought a sense of peace and understanding to my cosmic journey. I carry the tranquility of your teachings as I continue to dance through the realms of the grand tapestry. May the Hanged Harmony guide my steps."

The Keeper of the Hanged Harmony, their eyes reflecting the timeless tranquility, nodded in acknowledgment. "May the cosmic dance unfold with the magic of surrender. Go forth, seeker, and let the Hanged Harmony carry you to realms yet unveiled."

Leaving the realm of the Hanged Harmony, the Fool felt the peaceful energy lingering in his every step. The misty veil whispered tales of surrender's dance, and the fragrance of cosmic blossoms accompanied him toward the next archway. The rhythmic dance of the cosmic tapestry echoed in his heart, and the Keeper's tranquil teachings illuminated his path as he ventured into the uncharted territories that awaited in the chapters yet to unfold.

As the Fool traversed through the mystical landscapes, a gentle breeze carried wisps of insight to him. The suspended figure in the Hanged Harmony realm had left an imprint on his understanding, urging him to embrace the beauty of release and trust in the cosmic currents that guided his journey.

The Fool's heart resonated with the stillness of surrender, and he found solace in the simplicity of letting go. The dance of the Hanged Harmony had taught him that sometimes, wisdom emerges not in resistance but in the serenity of yielding to the flow of existence.

With each step, the Fool felt a newfound lightness, unburdened by the weight of unnecessary attachments. The cosmic tapestry seemed to respond to his surrendered steps, weaving a melody of harmonious energies around him. The lessons of the Hanged Harmony lingered like a gentle echo, inviting him to carry the magic of surrender into the realms yet to be explored.

As the Fool approached the next archway, he marvelled at the transformative power of surrender. The cosmic dance, with its ever-changing rhythms, held the promise of revelations and growth. With gratitude in his heart, the Fool stepped into the unknown, guided by the serenity of the Hanged Harmony and eager to discover the enchantments that awaited in the chapters yet to unfold.

~ Fourteen ~

CHAPTER 14: THE SHROUDED PASSAGE

The Fool stepped into the next realm, and an eerie stillness greeted him. The air was heavy with a sense of impending transformation, and shadows danced in mysterious patterns. In the heart of this enigmatic space, a figure shrouded in a cloak approached, their eyes gleaming with otherworldly wisdom.

"Greetings, seeker of the cosmic dance. I am the Guardian of the Shrouded Passage, where the magic of death and rebirth weaves through the cosmic tapestry," the figure intoned, their voice a haunting melody that resonated with the echoes of eternity.

The Fool, feeling the weight of the solemn atmosphere, bowed respectfully. "Great Guardian of the Shrouded Passage, I come with a heart open to the mysteries of transformation. The dance has led me to your realm, and I seek to understand the enchantments woven within the grand tapestry."

The Guardian of the Shrouded Passage acknowledged the Fool's presence with a nod, their eyes reflecting the depth of ancient knowledge. "In this realm, seeker, we explore the magic of death and rebirth, where shadows give way to new beginnings. What questions stir within your heart as you step into the dance of eternal transformation?"

Eager to unravel the secrets of this shadowed space, the Fool spoke, "Great Guardian, I wish to comprehend the nature of death in the cosmic dance. How does one navigate the darkness and embrace the promise of rebirth? What wisdom guides the seeker in understanding the enchantments of the Shrouded Passage?"

The Guardian spoke of death as a cosmic transition, emphasising the transformative power that lies in the embrace of shadows. "In the dance of death and rebirth, seeker, navigate the shadows with a heart unburdened by fear. Embrace the darkness, for the Shrouded Passage unfolds when you release attachments to the old. Trust in the cosmic currents of transformation, and let your journey be an eternal dance with the mysteries of existence."

Inspired by the Guardian's words, the Fool posed another question, "Great Guardian, how does one attune themselves to the cosmic energies of rebirth? What wisdom guides the seeker in aligning with the transformative currents that flow through the Shrouded Passage?"

The Guardian spoke of cosmic attunement, encouraging the Fool to become attuned to the energies of renewal. "In the realm of rebirth, seeker, attune yourself to the cosmic energies. Feel the transformative currents that flow through the Shrouded Passage, and let your steps be in harmony with the cosmic dance of renewal. Align with the rebirth of life, and become a conscious partner in the eternal dance of transformation."

As the conversation unfolded, the Fool felt a shadowed energy enveloping him. The realm, with its cloaked figure and the Guardian as a guide, became a sanctuary where the dance of death revealed itself as a tapestry woven with threads of eternal transformation.

"Great Guardian, how does one invoke the magic of letting go in the cosmic dance of death? What wisdom guides the seeker in releasing attachments and surrendering to the inevitability of change?" the Fool inquired, aware of the profound release that often accompanied the dance of shadows.

The Guardian acknowledged the intertwining dance of death and letting go, speaking of the importance of surrender to the cosmic currents. "In the cosmic dance of letting go, seeker, release attachments as the shadows unfold. Embrace the inevitability of change, for in the Shrouded Passage, the old must yield to the new. Surrender to the cosmic currents of transformation, and let the shadows guide your steps through the eternal symphony."

Feeling the shadowed energies resonating within him, the Fool delved deeper into the conversation. "Great Guardian, how does one navigate the challenges of facing the unknown in the cosmic dance of death? What wisdom guides the seeker in confronting the mysteries with courage and resilience?"

The Guardian spoke of the challenges inherent in the dance of death, encouraging the Fool to face the unknown with courage. "In the realm of challenges, seeker, navigate the dance of death with courage. Confront the mysteries as gateways to new beginnings, and let your journey through the shadows be a testament to your resilience. Face the unknown with the strength of the Shrouded Passage, and let the shadows guide your steps through the eternal symphony."

As the moonlit conversation between the Fool and the Guardian continued, the realm seemed to glow with a shadowed energy. The cloaked figure, now a symbol of eternal transformation, became a vessel of cosmic renewal where the dance unfolded with haunting precision.

"Great Guardian, what role does acceptance play in the cosmic dance of death? How does one foster peace amidst the inevitable transitions, embracing the magic of surrender in the Shrouded Passage?" the Fool inquired, sensing the profound connection between death and acceptance.

The Guardian spoke of acceptance as the soul's melody in the dance of death, urging the Fool to weave threads of peace into the cosmic tapestry. "In the realm of death, let acceptance be the enchanting thread that binds the soul to serenity. Foster peace amidst transitions, and let the dance of death be a testament to the magic of surrender. Through the Shrouded Passage, you shall contribute to the haunting symphony of cosmic transformation."

Expressing his gratitude, the Fool said, "Great Guardian, your wisdom has brought a sense of shadowed enlightenment to my cosmic journey. I carry the echoes of your teachings as I continue to dance through the realms of the grand tapestry. May the Shrouded Passage guide my steps."

The Guardian of the Shrouded Passage, their eyes reflecting the depth of cosmic transitions, nodded in acknowledgment. "May the cosmic dance unfold with the magic of death's eternal symphony. Go forth, seeker, and let the shadows of the Shrouded Passage carry you to realms yet unveiled."

Leaving the realm of the Shrouded Passage, the Fool felt the shadowed energy lingering in his every step. The mystery of death's dance whispered tales of renewal, and the fragrance of withering blossoms accompanied him toward the next archway. The rhythmic dance of the cosmic tapestry echoed in his heart, and the Guardian's haunting teachings illuminated his path as he ventured into the uncharted territories that awaited in the chapters yet to unfold.

As the Fool stepped away from the Shrouded Passage, a subtle heaviness lingered in the air, like the remnants of a haunting melody. The encounter with the Guardian of Death had left an indelible mark on his spirit. The cosmic dance, once vibrant and full of wonder, now bore the weight of inevitable transformations.

The Fool's heart, while still open to the mysteries that lay ahead, carried the shadows of the encounter. The spectre of death had woven threads of introspection into the tapestry of his being. The awareness of life's impermanence and the inevitability of change cast a solemn hue over his once carefree steps.

As he continued through the mystical realms, the Fool found himself reflecting on the delicate balance between existence and the void. The echoes of the Guardian's wisdom resonated within him, urging him to contemplate the significance of each step in the cosmic dance.

The landscape around him seemed to mirror the shifting emotions within. Withered blossoms whispered tales of both loss and renewal, and the cosmic tapestry appeared to shimmer with a more profound, albeit somber, brilliance.

The Fool's companionship with the white dog took on a poignant quality. The loyal creature, sensing the shift in energy, walked faithfully by his side, its eyes reflecting a silent understanding of the weight carried by the Fool.

The once carefree optimism that marked the early steps of his journey had transformed into a more nuanced understanding of the cosmic dance. The Fool grappled with the paradox of life and death, feeling both the melancholy of what was lost and the potential for new beginnings that lay in the shadows.

Yet, amidst the contemplation and the shadowed atmosphere, a spark of resilience flickered in the Fool's eyes. The encounter with death had not extinguished his spirit but had rather ignited a deeper awareness. The dance continued, and with each step, the Fool carried the echoes of the Shrouded Passage, a reminder that in every end, there is the promise of a new beginning.

The cosmic tapestry unfolded before him, a canvas of mysteries waiting to be explored. The Fool, now a more seasoned traveler, moved forward with a blend of reverence for the past and a tempered optimism for the unknown realms that awaited. The rhythmic dance of the cosmic tapestry echoed in his heart, a symphony that harmonised both the light and the shadows within.

~ Fifteen ~

CHAPTER 15: THE ALCHEMICAL BALANCE

The Fool stepped into the next realm, and a serene energy enveloped him. The air shimmered with iridescence, and a gentle river flowed through the heart of this ethereal space. Standing by the riverbanks was a figure, cloaked in flowing robes, blending hues of gold and silver. Their presence radiated a tranquil wisdom that seemed to harmonise with the cosmic currents.

"Greetings, seeker of the cosmic dance. I am the Keeper of Alchemical Balance, where the magic of harmony and transformation weaves through the cosmic tapestry," the figure greeted, their voice a melodic whisper that echoed the rhythmic flow of the river.

The Fool, captivated by the serenity of the surroundings, bowed respectfully. "Great Keeper of Alchemical Balance, I come with a heart open to the mysteries of harmony. The dance has led me to your realm, and I seek to understand the enchantments woven within the grand tapestry."

The Keeper of Alchemical Balance acknowledged the Fool's presence with a nod, their eyes reflecting the shimmering river's gentle ebb and flow. "In this realm, seeker, we explore the magic of temperance, where the blending of elements creates a symphony of transformation. What questions stir within your heart as you step into the dance of alchemical harmony?"

Eager to unravel the secrets of this luminous space, the Fool spoke, "Great Keeper, I wish to comprehend the nature of temperance in the cosmic dance. How does one find balance amidst the ever-changing elements, and what wisdom guides the seeker in understanding the enchantments of the Alchemical Balance?"

The Keeper spoke of temperance as a cosmic alchemy, emphasising the transformative power that lies in the harmonious blending of opposing forces. "In the dance of temperance, seeker, find balance in the alchemy of opposites. Embrace the ever-changing elements, for the Alchemical Balance unfolds when you harmonise the forces within and without. Trust in the cosmic currents of transformation, and let your journey be a harmonious dance with the mysteries of existence."

Inspired by the Keeper's words, the Fool posed another question, "Great Keeper, how does one attune themselves to the cosmic energies of alchemical harmony? What wisdom guides the seeker in aligning with the transformative currents that flow through the Alchemical Balance?"

The Keeper spoke of cosmic attunement, encouraging the Fool to become attuned to the energies of equilibrium. "In the realm of alchemical harmony, seeker, attune yourself to the cosmic energies. Feel the transformative currents that flow through the Alchemical Balance, and let your steps be in harmony with the cosmic dance of equilibrium. Align with the balance of life's elements, and become a conscious partner in the alchemical dance of transformation."

As the conversation unfolded, the Fool felt a luminous energy enveloping him. The realm, with its flowing river and the Keeper as a guide, became a sanctuary where the dance of temperance revealed itself as a tapestry woven with threads of harmonious transformation.

"Great Keeper, how does one invoke the magic of adaptation in the cosmic dance of temperance? What wisdom guides the seeker in embracing change and adapting to the ebb and flow of the

Alchemical Balance?" the Fool inquired, aware of the fluid nature that often accompanied the dance of equilibrium.

The Keeper acknowledged the intertwining dance of temperance and adaptation, speaking of the importance of embracing change with grace. "In the cosmic dance of adaptation, seeker, embrace change as a natural element of the Alchemical Balance. Adapt to the ebb and flow of life's currents, for in temperance, the dance is enriched by your ability to flow with the cosmic energies. Let adaptation guide your steps through the harmonious symphony."

Feeling the luminous energies resonating within him, the Fool delved deeper into the conversation. "Great Keeper, how does one navigate the challenges of maintaining inner harmony in the cosmic dance of

temperance? What wisdom guides the seeker in facing the conflicts within and without with equanimity?"

The Keeper spoke of the challenges inherent in the dance of temperance, encouraging the Fool to seek inner harmony amidst conflicts. "In the realm of challenges, seeker, navigate the dance of temperance with inner harmony. Face conflicts as opportunities for inner alchemy, and let your journey through the Alchemical Balance be a testament to your equanimity. Find balance within, and let the cosmic symphony harmonise the forces without."

As the moonlit conversation between the Fool and the Keeper continued, the realm seemed to glow with a luminous energy. The flowing river, now a symbol of temperance's fluid grace, became a vessel of cosmic equilibrium where the dance unfolded with serene precision.

"Great Keeper, what role does patience play in the cosmic dance of temperance? How does one cultivate patience and allow the alchemical processes to unfold in their own time?" the Fool inquired, sensing the profound connection between temperance and the virtue of patience.

The Keeper spoke of patience as the heartbeat in the dance of temperance, urging the Fool to weave threads of patience into the cosmic tapestry. "In the realm of temperance, let patience be the enchanting thread that binds the dance together. Cultivate patience and allow the alchemical processes to unfold in their own time. Through the Alchemical Balance, you shall contribute to the harmonious symphony of cosmic transformation."

Expressing his gratitude, the Fool said, "Great Keeper, your wisdom has brought a sense of luminous balance to my cosmic journey. I carry the radiance of your teachings as I continue to dance through the realms of the grand tapestry. May the Alchemical Balance guide my steps."

The Keeper of Alchemical Balance, their eyes reflecting the shimmering river's timeless ebb and flow, nodded in acknowledgment. "May the cosmic dance unfold with the magic of temperance's luminous symphony. Go forth, seeker, and let the Alchemical Balance carry you to realms yet unveiled."

Leaving the realm of the Alchemical Balance, the Fool felt the luminous energy lingering in his every step. The dance of temperance whispered tales of equilibrium, and the fragrance of blooming blossoms accompanied him toward the next archway. The rhythmic dance of the cosmic tapestry echoed in his heart, and the Keeper's luminous teachings illuminated his path as he ventured into the uncharted territories that awaited in the chapters yet to unfold.

$$\sim \text{Sixteen} \sim$$

CHAPTER 16: THE SHADOWED CHAINS

The Fool stepped through the archway into a realm veiled in obsidian shadows. The air was thick with a mysterious energy, and ominous whispers echoed through the darkened space. In the centre stood a figure, cloaked in darkness, with horns that curled towards the starless sky. The eyes of the Devil glowed with an unsettling intensity, and the air seemed to vibrate with an eerie resonance.

"Greetings, seeker of the cosmic dance. I am the Keeper of Shadowed Chains, where the magic of entanglement and liberation weaves through the cosmic tapestry," the Devil intoned, their voice a seductive murmur that echoed the entwining shadows.

The Fool, feeling the weight of the shadowed atmosphere, bowed cautiously. "Great Keeper of Shadowed Chains, I come with a heart open to the mysteries of entanglement. The dance has led me to your realm, and I seek to understand the enchantments woven within the grand tapestry."

The Devil acknowledged the Fool's presence with a sly grin, their eyes reflecting the intricate web of entangled energies. "In this realm, seeker, we explore the magic of binding and liberation, where the dance is woven with threads of desire and restraint.

What questions stir within your heart as you step into the entangled dance?"

Eager to unravel the secrets of this shadowed space, the Fool spoke, "Great Keeper, I wish to comprehend the nature of entanglement in the cosmic dance. How does one navigate the seductive allure of desires and the constraining chains, and what wisdom guides the seeker in understanding the enchantments of the Shadowed Chains?"

The Devil spoke of entanglement as a cosmic dance of desires and restraint, emphasising the transformative power that lies in the delicate balance between freedom and captivity. "In the dance of entanglement, seeker, navigate the seductive allure with a discerning heart. Embrace desires, for the Shadowed Chains unfold when you understand the intricate dance between freedom and restraint. Trust in the cosmic currents of transformation, and let your journey be a captivating dance with the mysteries of existence."

Inspired by the Devil's words, the Fool posed another question, "Great Keeper, how does one attune themselves to the cosmic energies of liberation in the dance of entanglement? What wisdom guides the seeker in aligning with the transformative currents that flow through the Shadowed Chains?"

The Devil spoke of cosmic attunement, encouraging the Fool to become attuned to the energies of both desire and liberation. "In the realm of entanglement, seeker, attune yourself to the cosmic energies. Feel the transformative currents that flow through the Shadowed Chains, and let your steps be in harmony with the cosmic dance of desires and liberation. Align with the freedom within the chains, and become a conscious partner in the entangled dance of transformation."

As the conversation unfolded, the Fool felt a shadowed energy enveloping him. The realm, with its entwining shadows and the Devil as a guide, became a labyrinth where the dance of entanglement revealed itself as a tapestry woven with threads of seduction and release.

"Great Keeper, how does one invoke the magic of self-awareness in the cosmic dance of entanglement? What wisdom guides the seeker in understanding their desires and navigating the complexities of the Shadowed Chains?" the Fool inquired, aware of the intricate dance that often accompanied the entanglement of desires.

The Devil acknowledged the intertwining dance of entanglement and self-awareness, speaking of the importance of understanding one's desires. "In the cosmic dance of self-awareness, seeker, embrace the intricacies of your desires. Navigate the complexities of the Shadowed Chains with awareness, for in entanglement, the dance is enriched by your understanding of the seductive threads that bind you. Let self-awareness guide your steps through the captivating symphony."

Feeling the shadowed energies resonating within him, the Fool delved deeper into the conversation. "Great Keeper, how does one navigate the challenges of breaking free from oppressive entanglements in the cosmic dance? What wisdom guides the seeker in liberating themselves from the constraining chains that bind them?"

The Devil spoke of the challenges inherent in the dance of entanglement, encouraging the Fool to break free with resilience. "In the realm of challenges, seeker, navigate the dance of liberation with resilience. Break free from oppressive entanglements and let your journey through the Shadowed Chains be a testament to your strength. Liberation is found in the conscious unraveling of the seductive threads that bind. Face the entanglements with the wisdom of the captivating symphony."

As the moonlit conversation between the Fool and the Devil continued, the realm seemed to pulse with a shadowed energy. The entwining shadows, now a symbol of desires and liberation, became a vessel of cosmic seduction where the dance unfolded with entrancing precision.

"Great Keeper, what role does surrender play in the cosmic dance of entanglement? How does one foster acceptance amidst the seductive allure and find liberation through surrender in the

Shadowed Chains?" the Fool inquired, sensing the profound connection between entanglement and the virtue of surrender.

The Devil spoke of surrender as the key to liberation in the dance of entanglement, urging the Fool to weave threads of acceptance into the cosmic tapestry. "In the realm of surrender, seeker, let acceptance be the enchanting thread that binds you to liberation. Foster surrender amidst the seductive allure, and let the dance of the Shadowed Chains be a testament to the magic of letting go. Through surrender, you shall contribute to the captivating symphony of cosmic transformation."

Expressing his gratitude, the Fool said, "Great Keeper, your wisdom has brought a sense of shadowed allure to my cosmic journey. I carry the echoes of your teachings as I continue to dance through the realms of the grand tapestry. May the Shadowed Chains guide my steps."

The Devil, their eyes reflecting the intricate dance of desires and liberation, nodded in acknowledgment. "May the cosmic dance unfold with the magic of entanglement's captivating symphony. Go forth, seeker, and let the Shadowed Chains carry you to realms yet unveiled."

Leaving the realm of the Shadowed Chains, the Fool felt the shadowed energy lingering in his every step. The seductive dance whispered tales of desires and liberation, and the fragrance of temptation.

~ Seventeen ~

CHAPTER 17: THE TOWER OF THUNDER

The Fool traversed through the archway into a realm engulfed in the tempest's fury. The air crackled with electric energy, and the sky, once serene, now roared with thunder. In the midst of the storm stood the Tower of Thunder, a towering structure shattered and broken—the remnants of what once might have been a bastion of stability. A figure, cloaked in tattered robes, emerged from the rubble, their eyes reflecting the chaos that echoed through the Shattered Tower.

"Greetings, seeker of the cosmic dance. I am the Warden of the Tower of Thunder, where the magic of upheaval and reconstruction weaves through the cosmic tapestry," the Warden declared, their voice resonating with the echoes of falling debris.

The Fool, feeling the turbulence in the atmosphere, bowed in acknowledgment. "Great Warden of the Tower of Thunder, I come with a heart open to the mysteries of upheaval. The dance has led me to your realm, and I seek to understand the enchantments woven within the grand tapestry."

The Warden acknowledged the Fool's presence with a stoic gaze, their eyes reflecting the shattered fragments that surrounded them. "In this realm, seeker, we explore the magic of destruction and renewal, where the dance is forged from the remnants of fallen structures. What questions stir within your heart as you step into the tumultuous dance?"

Eager to unravel the secrets of this turbulent space, the Fool spoke, "Great Warden, I wish to comprehend the nature of upheaval in the cosmic dance. How does one navigate the chaos of destruction and find the spark of renewal amidst the shattered remnants, and what wisdom guides the seeker in understanding the enchantments of the Tower of Thunder?"

The Warden spoke of upheaval as a cosmic force of deconstruction and reconstruction, emphasising the transformative power that lies in embracing change and finding renewal in the midst of chaos. "In the dance of upheaval, seeker, navigate the chaos with an unyielding spirit. Embrace destruction, for the Tower of Thunder unfolds when you find the resilience to rebuild amidst the fallen structures. Trust in the cosmic currents of transformation, and let your journey be a tumultuous dance with the mysteries of existence."

Inspired by the Warden's words, the Fool posed another question, "Great Warden, how does one attune themselves to the cosmic energies of renewal in the dance of upheaval? What wisdom guides the seeker in aligning with the transformative currents that flow through the Tower of Thunder?"

The Warden spoke of cosmic attunement, encouraging the Fool to become attuned to the energies of both destruction and reconstruction. "In the realm of upheaval, seeker, attune yourself to the cosmic energies. Feel the transformative currents that flow through the Tower of Thunder, and let your steps be in harmony with the cosmic dance of destruction and renewal. Align with the renewal amidst the ruins, and become a conscious partner in the tumultuous dance of transformation."

As the conversation unfolded, the Fool felt a turbulent energy enveloping him. The realm, with its shattered tower and the Warden as a guide, became a chaotic arena where the dance of upheaval revealed itself as a tapestry woven with threads of destruction and rebirth.

"Great Warden, how does one invoke the magic of resilience in the cosmic dance of upheaval? What wisdom guides the seeker in standing firm amidst the storm and rebuilding from the shattered remnants?" the Fool inquired, aware of the strength required to endure the tumultuous dance.

The Warden acknowledged the intertwining dance of upheaval and resilience, speaking of the importance of standing firm in the face of chaos. "In the cosmic dance of resilience, seeker, stand firm amidst the storm. Rebuild from the shattered remnants with unwavering determination, for in upheaval, the dance is enriched by your ability to endure and reconstruct. Let resilience guide your steps through the tumultuous symphony."

Feeling the turbulent energies resonating within him, the Fool delved deeper into the conversation. "Great Warden, how does one navigate the challenges of letting go in the cosmic dance of upheaval? What wisdom guides the seeker in releasing attachments to the structures that crumble, and surrendering to the inevitability of change?"

The Warden spoke of the challenges inherent in the dance of upheaval, encouraging the Fool to release attachments with a heart unburdened by resistance. "In the realm of challenges, seeker, navigate the dance of letting go with grace. Release attachments to the structures that crumble, and surrender to the inevitability of change. The Tower of Thunder unfolds when you embrace the transformative currents with an open heart. Face the challenges with the wisdom of the tumultuous symphony."

As the thunderous conversation between the Fool and the Warden continued, the realm seemed to reverberate with a chaotic energy. The shattered tower, now a symbol of destruction and renewal, became a vessel of cosmic upheaval where the dance unfolded with turbulent precision.

"Great Warden, what role does acceptance play in the cosmic dance of upheaval? How does one foster peace amidst the storm and find solace in the acceptance of change within the Tower of Thunder?" the Fool inquired, sensing the profound connection between upheaval and the virtue of acceptance.

The Warden spoke of acceptance as the anchor in the dance of upheaval, urging the Fool to weave threads of peace into the cosmic tapestry. "In the realm of acceptance, seeker, let peace be the enchanting thread that binds you to the chaotic symphony. Foster acceptance amidst the storm, and let the dance of the Tower of Thunder be a testament to the magic of surrender. Through acceptance, you shall contribute to the tumultuous symphony of cosmic transformation."

Expressing his gratitude, the Fool said, "Great Warden, your wisdom has brought a sense of tumultuous renewal to my cosmic journey. I carry the echoes of your teachings as I continue to dance through the realms of the grand tapestry. May the Tower of Thunder guide my steps."

The Warden of the Tower of Thunder, their eyes reflecting the chaotic dance of destruction and renewal, nodded in acknowledgment. "May the cosmic dance unfold with the magic of upheaval's tumultuous symphony. Go forth, seeker, and let the Tower of Thunder carry you to realms yet unveiled."

Leaving the realm of the Tower of Thunder, the Fool felt the turbulent energy lingering in his every step. The dance of upheaval whispered tales of destruction and rebirth, and the thunderous echoes of fallen structures accompanied him toward the next archway. The rhythmic dance of the cosmic tapestry echoed in his heart, and the Warden's tumultuous teachings illuminated his path as he ventured into the uncharted territories that awaited in the chapters yet to unfold.

~ Eighteen ~

CHAPTER 18: CELESTIAL REVERIE

The Fool, having passed through the archway, found himself in a realm adorned with an ethereal glow. The air sparkled with the luminescence of a thousand stars, and the sky stretched into an endless celestial canvas. In the centre of this cosmic haven stood a figure, radiant and serene, surrounded by a celestial aura. The Star, as she introduced herself, beckoned the Fool to approach with a gentle wave.

"Greetings, seeker of the cosmic dance. I am the Guardian of Celestial Reverie, where the magic of stardust and dreams weaves through the cosmic tapestry," the Star declared, her voice a melodic whisper echoing through the astral expanse.

The Fool, enchanted by the celestial beauty around him, bowed respectfully. "Great Guardian of Celestial Reverie, I come with a heart open to the mysteries of stardust. The dance has led me to your realm, and I seek to understand the enchantments woven within the grand tapestry."

The Star acknowledged the Fool's presence with a radiant smile, her eyes reflecting the cosmos within. "In this realm, seeker, we explore the magic of dreams and the celestial dance, where stardust illuminates the cosmic tapestry. What questions stir within your heart as you step into this celestial reverie?"

Eager to unravel the secrets of this ethereal space, the Fool spoke, "Great Guardian, I wish to comprehend the nature of stardust in the cosmic dance. How does one connect with the celestial energies and harness the magic of dreams within the cosmic tapestry, and what wisdom guides the seeker in understanding the enchantments of Celestial Reverie?"

The Star spoke of stardust as the essence of dreams and cosmic connection, emphasising the transformative power that lies in embracing the ethereal realm of possibilities. "In the dance of stardust, seeker, connect with the celestial energies with an open heart. Embrace the magic of dreams, for Celestial Reverie unfolds when you allow the stardust to illuminate your cosmic journey. Trust in the astral currents of transformation, and let your dance be a celestial waltz through the mysteries of existence."

Inspired by the Star's words, the Fool posed another question, "Great Guardian, how does one attune themselves to the cosmic energies of dreams in the dance of stardust? What wisdom guides the seeker in aligning with the transformative currents that flow through Celestial Reverie?"

The Star spoke of cosmic attunement, encouraging the Fool to become attuned to the energies of dreams and the celestial dance. "In the realm of stardust, seeker, attune yourself to the cosmic energies. Feel the transformative currents that flow through Celestial Reverie, and let your steps be in harmony with the celestial dance of dreams. Align with the magic of possibility, and become a conscious partner in the ethereal dance of transformation."

As the conversation unfolded, the Fool felt a celestial energy enveloping him. The realm, with its twinkling stars and the Star as a guide, became a celestial expanse where the dance of stardust revealed itself as a tapestry woven with threads of dreams and cosmic connection.

"Great Guardian, how does one invoke the magic of inspiration in the cosmic dance of stardust? What wisdom guides the seeker in embracing the creative flow and allowing inspiration to guide their steps through Celestial Reverie?" the Fool inquired, aware of the boundless inspiration that often accompanied the dance of stardust.

The Star acknowledged the intertwining dance of stardust and inspiration, speaking of the importance of embracing the creative flow. "In the cosmic dance of inspiration, seeker, embrace the creative currents. Allow stardust to kindle the flames of inspiration within you, for in Celestial Reverie, the dance is enriched by your ability to create and manifest. Let inspiration guide your steps through the celestial symphony."

Feeling the celestial energies resonating within him, the Fool delved deeper into the conversation. "Great Guardian, how does one navigate the challenges of staying grounded in the cosmic dance of stardust? What wisdom guides the seeker in balancing the ethereal dreams with a rooted connection to reality within Celestial Reverie?"

The Star spoke of the challenges inherent in the dance of stardust, encouraging the Fool to maintain a balance between dreams and reality. "In the realm of challenges, seeker, navigate the dance with a grounded spirit. Balance the ethereal dreams with a rooted connection to reality, for Celestial Reverie unfolds when you find harmony between the celestial and the earthly. Face the challenges with the wisdom of the celestial symphony."

As the moonlit conversation between the Fool and the Star continued, the realm seemed to shimmer with a celestial energy. The twinkling stars, now a symbol of dreams and cosmic connection, became a vessel of cosmic inspiration where the dance unfolded with enchanting precision.

"Great Guardian, what role does gratitude play in the cosmic dance of stardust? How does one foster appreciation for the cosmic blessings and find fulfilment in the acknowledgment of the gifts within Celestial Reverie?" the Fool inquired, sensing the profound connection between stardust and the virtue of gratitude.

The Star spoke of gratitude as the guiding light in the dance of stardust, urging the Fool to weave threads of appreciation into the cosmic tapestry. "In the realm of gratitude, seeker, let appreciation be the enchanting thread that binds you to the celestial symphony. Foster gratitude for the cosmic blessings, and let the dance of Celestial Reverie be a testament to the magic of acknowledging the gifts. Through gratitude, you shall contribute to the enchanting symphony of cosmic transformation."

Expressing his gratitude, the Fool said, "Great Guardian, your wisdom has brought a sense of celestial wonder to my cosmic journey. I carry the echoes of your teachings as I continue to dance through the realms of the grand tapestry. May Celestial Reverie guide my steps."

The Star, her eyes reflecting the cosmic dance of dreams and connection, nodded in acknowledgment. "May the cosmic dance unfold with the magic of stardust's celestial symphony. Go forth, seeker, and let Celestial Reverie carry you to realms yet unveiled."

Leaving the realm of Celestial Reverie, the Fool felt the celestial energy lingering in his every step. The dance of stardust whispered tales of dreams and cosmic connection, and the twinkling stars accompanied him toward the next archway. The rhythmic dance of the cosmic tapestry echoed in his heart, and the Star's celestial teachings illuminated his path as he ventured into the uncharted territories that awaited in the chapters yet to unfold.

~ Nineteen ~

CHAPTER 19: LUNAR
ENCHANTMENT

As the Fool stepped through the archway, he found himself in a realm bathed in the silvery glow of moonlight. The air carried a mystic allure, and the landscape seemed to shift with the phases of an unseen celestial dance. In the midst of this lunar enchantment stood the Moon, a figure cloaked in luminescence, her presence emanating an otherworldly charm. With a graceful gesture, she invited the Fool to approach.

"Greetings, seeker of the cosmic dance. I am the Weaver of Lunar Enchantment, where the magic of moonlight and illusions weaves through the cosmic tapestry," the Moon whispered, her voice a soft serenade echoing through the nocturnal expanse.

The Fool, captivated by the ethereal beauty around him, bowed respectfully. "Great Weaver of Lunar Enchantment, I come with a heart open to the mysteries of moonlight. The dance has led me to your realm, and I seek to understand the enchantments woven within the grand tapestry."

The Moon acknowledged the Fool's presence with a radiant smile, her eyes reflecting the ebb and flow of tides within. "In this realm, seeker, we explore the magic of illusions and the dance of shadows, where moonlight illuminates the cosmic tapestry. What questions stir within your heart as you step into this lunar enchantment?"

Eager to unravel the secrets of this mystical space, the Fool spoke, "Great Weaver, I wish to comprehend the nature of moonlight in the cosmic dance. How does one embrace the illusions and navigate the dance of shadows within the cosmic tapestry, and what wisdom guides the seeker in understanding the enchantments of Lunar Enchantment?"

The Moon spoke of moonlight as the veil between reality and illusion, emphasising the transformative power that lies in embracing the unseen mysteries. "In the dance of moonlight, seeker, embrace the illusions with an open mind. Navigate the dance of shadows, for Lunar Enchantment unfolds when you allow the moonlight to reveal

the hidden truths. Trust in the nocturnal currents of transformation, and let your dance be a lunar waltz through the mysteries of existence."

Inspired by the Moon's words, the Fool posed another question, "Great Weaver, how does one attune themselves to the cosmic energies of illusions in the dance of moonlight? What wisdom guides the seeker in aligning with the transformative currents that flow through Lunar Enchantment?"

The Moon spoke of cosmic attunement, encouraging the Fool to become attuned to the energies of illusions and the dance of shadows. "In the realm of moonlight, seeker, attune yourself to the cosmic energies. Feel the transformative currents that flow through Lunar Enchantment, and let your steps be in harmony with the lunar dance of illusions. Align with the magic of mystery, and become a conscious partner in the nocturnal dance of transformation."

As the conversation unfolded, the Fool felt a lunar energy enveloping him. The realm, with its shifting shadows and the Moon as a guide, became a mystical landscape where the dance of moonlight revealed itself as a tapestry woven with threads of illusions and hidden truths.

"Great Weaver, how does one invoke the magic of intuition in the cosmic dance of moonlight? What wisdom guides the seeker in embracing the intuitive flow and allowing insights to guide their steps through Lunar Enchantment?" the Fool inquired, aware of the profound intuition often associated with the dance of moonlight.

The Moon acknowledged the intertwining dance of moonlight and intuition, speaking of the importance of embracing the intuitive flow. "In the cosmic dance of intuition, seeker, embrace the intuitive currents. Allow moonlight to illuminate the path of insight within you, for in Lunar Enchantment, the dance is enriched by your ability to listen to the whispers of the night. Let intuition guide your steps through the lunar symphony."

Feeling the lunar energies resonating within him, the Fool delved deeper into the conversation. "Great Weaver, how does one navigate the challenges of facing one's fears in the cosmic dance of moonlight? What wisdom guides the seeker in confronting the shadows and finding courage within Lunar Enchantment?"

The Moon spoke of the challenges inherent in the dance of moonlight, encouraging the Fool to confront fears with courage. "In the realm of challenges, seeker, navigate the dance with a courageous spirit. Confront the shadows, for Lunar Enchantment unfolds when you face your fears and find strength within the nocturnal mysteries. Face the challenges with the wisdom of the lunar symphony."

As the starlit conversation between the Fool and the Moon continued, the realm seemed to shimmer with a lunar energy. The shifting shadows, now a symbol of illusions and hidden truths, became a vessel of cosmic intuition where the dance unfolded with enchanting precision.

"Great Weaver, what role does reflection play in the cosmic dance of moonlight? How does one foster introspection and find clarity in the reflection of the moon within Lunar Enchantment?" the Fool inquired, sensing the profound connection between moonlight and the virtue of reflection.

The Moon spoke of reflection as the gentle glow in the dance of moonlight, urging the Fool to weave threads of introspection into the cosmic tapestry. "In the realm of reflection, seeker, let introspection be the enchanting thread that binds you to the lunar symphony. Foster clarity in the reflection of the moon, and let the dance of Lunar Enchantment be a testament to the magic of inner contemplation. Through reflection, you shall contribute to the enchanting symphony of cosmic transformation."

Expressing his gratitude, the Fool said, "Great Weaver, your wisdom has brought a sense of lunar wonder to my cosmic journey. I carry the echoes of your teachings as I continue to dance through the realms of the grand tapestry. May Lunar Enchantment guide my steps."

The Moon, her eyes reflecting the ebb and flow of tides within, nodded in acknowledgment. "May the cosmic dance unfold with the magic of moonlight's lunar symphony. Go forth, seeker, and let Lunar Enchantment carry you to realms yet unveiled."

Leaving the realm of Lunar Enchantment, the Fool felt the lunar energy lingering in his every step. The dance of moonlight whispered tales of illusions and hidden truths, and the shifting shadows accompanied him toward the next archway. The rhythmic dance of the cosmic tapestry echoed in his heart, and the Moon's mystical teachings illuminated his path as he ventured into the uncharted territories that awaited in the chapters yet to unfold.

~ Twenty ~

CHAPTER 20: RADIANT RESPLENDENCE

Emerging from the moonlit archway, the Fool found himself bathed in the warm, golden glow of a celestial dawn. The air was alive with the vibrant energy of a new day, and the landscape bloomed with resplendent hues. In the midst of this radiant realm stood the Sun, a figure emanating an effulgent brilliance that seemed to infuse life into every corner of the cosmic tapestry. With a beaming smile, the Sun welcomed the Fool to approach.

"Salutations, seeker of the cosmic dance. I am the Illuminator of Radiant Resplendence, where the magic of sunlight and vitality weaves through the cosmic tapestry," the Sun exclaimed, her voice a joyous melody echoing through the luminous expanse.

The Fool, uplifted by the radiant beauty around him, bowed respectfully. "Great Illuminator of Radiant Resplendence, I come with a heart open to the mysteries of sunlight. The dance has led me to your realm, and I seek to understand the enchantments woven within the grand tapestry."

The Sun acknowledged the Fool's presence with a warm embrace of light, her eyes reflecting the brilliance of a thousand suns. "In this realm, seeker, we explore the magic of vitality and the dance of illumination, where sunlight breathes life into the cosmic tapestry.

What questions stir within your heart as you step into this radiant resplendence?"

Eager to unravel the secrets of this luminous space, the Fool spoke, "Great Illuminator, I wish to comprehend the nature of sunlight in the cosmic dance. How does one bask in the vitality and dance with the illumination within the cosmic tapestry, and what wisdom guides the seeker in understanding the enchantments of Radiant Resplendence?"

The Sun spoke of sunlight as the source of life and illumination, emphasising the transformative power that lies in embracing the radiant energy. "In the dance of sunlight, seeker, bask in the vitality with an open spirit. Dance with the illumination, for Radiant Resplendence unfolds when you allow the sunlight to infuse vibrancy into your cosmic journey. Trust in the solar currents of transformation, and let your dance be a radiant waltz through the mysteries of existence."

Inspired by the Sun's words, the Fool posed another question, "Great Illuminator, how does one attune themselves to the cosmic energies of vitality in the dance of sunlight? What wisdom guides the seeker in aligning with the transformative currents that flow through Radiant Resplendence?"

The Sun spoke of cosmic attunement, encouraging the Fool to become attuned to the energies of vitality and the dance of illumination. "In the realm of sunlight, seeker, attune yourself to the cosmic energies. Feel the transformative currents that flow through Radiant Resplendence, and let your steps be in harmony with the solar dance of vitality. Align with the magic of life, and become a conscious partner in the luminous dance of transformation."

As the conversation unfolded, the Fool felt a solar energy enveloping him. The realm, with its golden radiance and the Sun as a guide, became a luminous landscape where the dance of sunlight revealed itself as a tapestry woven with threads of vitality and illumination.

"Great Illuminator, how does one invoke the magic of joy in the cosmic dance of sunlight? What wisdom guides the seeker in embracing the exuberance and allowing joy to guide their steps through Radiant Resplendence?" the Fool inquired, aware of the boundless joy often associated with the dance of sunlight.

The Sun acknowledged the intertwining dance of sunlight and joy, speaking of the importance of embracing the exuberance. "In the cosmic dance of joy, seeker, embrace the exuberant currents. Allow sunlight to fill your heart with joy, for in Radiant Resplendence, the dance is enriched by your ability to radiate happiness and positivity. Let joy guide your steps through the luminous symphony."

Feeling the solar energies resonating within him, the Fool delved deeper into the conversation. "Great Illuminator, how does one navigate the challenges of maintaining clarity in the cosmic dance of sunlight? What wisdom guides the seeker in staying focused and finding clarity within Radiant Resplendence?"

The Sun spoke of the challenges inherent in the dance of sunlight, encouraging the Fool to maintain focus with clarity. "In the realm of challenges, seeker, navigate the dance with a focused spirit. Maintain clarity, for Radiant Resplendence unfolds when you stay attuned to the radiant path and find focus within the luminous mysteries. Face the challenges with the wisdom of the solar symphony."

As the sunlit conversation between the Fool and the Sun continued, the realm seemed to shimmer with a solar energy. The golden radiance, now a symbol of vitality and illumination, became a vessel of cosmic joy where the dance unfolded with enchanting precision.

"Great Illuminator, what role does gratitude play in the cosmic dance of sunlight? How does one foster appreciation for the cosmic blessings and find fulfilment in the acknowledgment of the gifts within Radiant Resplendence?" the Fool inquired, sensing the profound connection between sunlight and the virtue of gratitude.

The Sun spoke of gratitude as the warmth in the dance of sunlight, urging the Fool to weave threads of appreciation into the cosmic tapestry. "In the realm of gratitude, seeker, let appreciation be the enchanting thread that binds you to the solar symphony. Foster gratitude for the cosmic blessings, and let the dance of Radiant Resplendence be a testament to the magic of acknowledging the gifts. Through gratitude, you shall contribute to the luminous symphony of cosmic transformation."

Expressing his gratitude, the Fool said, "Great Illuminator, your wisdom has brought a sense of solar wonder to my cosmic journey. I carry the echoes of your teachings as I continue to dance through the realms of the grand tapestry. May Radiant Resplendence guide my steps."

The Sun, her eyes reflecting the brilliance of a thousand suns, nodded in acknowledgment. "May the cosmic dance unfold with the magic of sunlight's luminous symphony. Go forth, seeker, and let Radiant Resplendence carry you to realms yet unveiled."

Leaving the realm of Radiant Resplendence, the Fool felt the solar energy lingering in his every step. The dance of sunlight whispered tales of vitality and illumination, and the golden radiance accompanied him toward the next archway. The rhythmic dance of the cosmic tapestry echoed in his heart, and the Sun's luminous teachings illuminated his path as he ventured into the uncharted territories that awaited in the chapters yet to unfold.

~ Twenty-One ~

CHAPTER 21: ETHEREAL JUDGMENT

Beyond the sun-kissed archway, the Fool entered a realm that seemed suspended between realms—a place where the air crackled with a mysterious energy. The atmosphere bore a weight of anticipation, and the landscape was painted in hues that shifted between twilight shadows and ethereal luminescence. In the centre of this enigmatic space stood the embodiment of Judgment, a figure veiled in mist, her presence radiating both solemnity and otherworldly authority.

"Greetings, seeker of the cosmic dance. I am the Arbiter of Ethereal Judgment, where the magic of decisions and consequences weaves through the cosmic tapestry," the Arbiter intoned, her voice echoing like distant echoes in a vast, cosmic chamber.

The Fool, sensing the gravity of the moment, bowed respectfully. "Great Arbiter of Ethereal Judgment, I come with a heart open to the mysteries of decisions and consequences. The dance has led me to your realm, and I seek to understand the enchantments woven within the grand tapestry."

The Arbiter acknowledged the Fool's presence with an enigmatic nod, her eyes veiled by the mist that surrounded her. "In this realm, seeker, we explore the magic of choices and the dance of accountability, where the echoes of decisions reverberate through the cosmic tapestry. What questions stir within your heart as you step into this ethereal judgment?"

Eager to unravel the secrets of this profound space, the Fool spoke, "Great Arbiter, I wish to comprehend the nature of decisions in the cosmic dance. How does one navigate the choices and dance with accountability within the cosmic tapestry, and what wisdom guides the seeker in understanding the enchantments of Ethereal Judgment?"

The Arbiter spoke of decisions as the threads that weave the fabric of fate, emphasising the transformative power that lies in embracing the consequences. "In the dance of decisions, seeker, navigate the choices with an open mind. Dance with accountability, for Ethereal Judgment unfolds when you allow the echoes of decisions to shape the tapestry of your cosmic journey. Trust in the nebulous currents of transformation, and let your dance be an ethereal waltz through the mysteries of existence."

Inspired by the Arbiter's words, the Fool posed another question, "Great Arbiter, how does one attune themselves to the cosmic energies of accountability in the dance of decisions? What wisdom guides the seeker in aligning with the transformative currents that flow through Ethereal Judgment?"

The Arbiter spoke of cosmic attunement, encouraging the Fool to become attuned to the energies of accountability and the dance of consequences. "In the realm of decisions, seeker, attune yourself to the cosmic energies. Feel the transformative currents that flow through Ethereal Judgment, and let your steps be in harmony with the judgmental dance of accountability. Align with the magic of consequences, and become a conscious partner in the ethereal dance of transformation."

As the conversation unfolded, the Fool felt a weighty energy enveloping him. The realm, with its shifting shadows and the Arbiter as a guide, became an enigmatic landscape where the dance of decisions revealed itself as a tapestry woven with threads of accountability and consequence.

"Great Arbiter, how does one invoke the magic of redemption in the cosmic dance of decisions? What wisdom guides the seeker in embracing the opportunity for redemption and allowing growth to guide their steps through Ethereal Judgment?" the Fool inquired, aware of the profound redemption often associated with the dance of decisions.

The Arbiter acknowledged the intertwining dance of decisions and redemption, speaking of the importance of embracing opportunities for growth. "In the cosmic dance of redemption, seeker, embrace the transformative currents. Allow decisions to be a path of redemption, for in Ethereal Judgment, the dance is enriched by your ability to learn, grow, and transcend. Let redemption guide your steps through the nebulous symphony."

Feeling the ethereal energies resonating within him, the Fool delved deeper into the conversation. "Great Arbiter, how does one navigate the challenges of facing the consequences of their decisions in the cosmic dance of Ethereal Judgment? What wisdom guides the seeker in finding resilience and facing the echoes within this enigmatic realm?"

The Arbiter spoke of the challenges inherent in the dance of decisions, encouraging the Fool to face consequences with resilience. "In the realm of challenges, seeker, navigate the dance with a resilient spirit. Face the consequences, for Ethereal Judgment unfolds when you confront the echoes of your decisions with strength and resilience. Face the challenges with the wisdom of the nebulous symphony."

As the enigmatic conversation between the Fool and the Arbiter continued, the realm seemed to shimmer with an ethereal energy. The shifting shadows, now a symbol of decisions and consequences, became a vessel of cosmic judgment where the dance unfolded with haunting precision.

"Great Arbiter, what role does reflection play in the cosmic dance of decisions? How does one foster introspection and find clarity in the reflection of their choices within Ethereal Judgment?" the Fool inquired, sensing the profound connection between decisions and the virtue of reflection.

The Arbiter spoke of reflection as the mist that veils the dance of decisions, urging the Fool to weave threads of introspection into the cosmic tapestry. "In the realm of reflection, seeker, let introspection be the enchanting mist that surrounds you in the ethereal symphony. Foster clarity in the reflection of your choices, and let the dance of Ethereal Judgment be a testament to the magic of inner contemplation. Through reflection, you shall contribute to the haunting symphony of cosmic transformation."

Expressing his gratitude, the Fool said, "Great Arbiter, your wisdom has brought a sense of ethereal wonder to my cosmic journey. I carry the echoes of your teachings as I continue to dance through the realms of the grand tapestry. May Ethereal Judgment guide my steps."

The Arbiter, her form veiled in mist, nodded in acknowledgment. "May the cosmic dance unfold with the magic of decisions' ethereal symphony. Go forth, seeker, and let Ethereal Judgment carry you to realms yet unveiled."

Leaving the realm of Ethereal Judgment, the Fool felt the ethereal energy lingering in his every step. The dance of decisions whispered tales of accountability and consequence, and the shifting shadows accompanied him toward the next archway. The rhythmic dance of the cosmic tapestry echoed in his heart, and the Arbiter's enigmatic teachings illuminated his path as he ventured into the uncharted territories that awaited in the chapters yet to unfold.

~ Twenty-Two ~

CHAPTER 22: COSMIC CULMINATION

Through the next archway, the Fool stepped into a realm that transcended the boundaries of time and space. The air pulsated with an energy that felt both ancient and timeless. The landscape unfolded like a kaleidoscope, showcasing the myriad facets of existence. At the centre of this cosmic culmination stood the World, a figure radiating a harmonious blend of elements—a living embodiment of the grand tapestry.

"Greetings, seeker of the cosmic dance. I am the Weaver of Cosmic Culmination, where the magic of synthesis and completion weaves through the cosmic tapestry," the World declared, her voice resonating like the symphony of the cosmos itself.

The Fool, humbled by the cosmic majesty around him, bowed respectfully. "Great Weaver of Cosmic Culmination, I come with a heart open to the mysteries of synthesis and completion. The dance has led me to your realm, and I seek to understand the enchantments woven within the grand tapestry."

The World acknowledged the Fool's presence with a gesture that seemed to encompass the entirety of creation. "In this realm, seeker, we explore the magic of unity and the dance of fulfilment, where the threads of existence weave into a seamless whole. What questions stir within your heart as you step into this cosmic culmination?"

Eager to unravel the secrets of this transcendent space, the Fool spoke, "Great Weaver, I wish to comprehend the nature of synthesis in the cosmic dance. How does one harmonise the diverse threads and dance with fulfilment within the cosmic tapestry, and what wisdom guides the seeker in understanding the enchantments of Cosmic Culmination?"

The World spoke of synthesis as the convergence of elements, emphasising the transformative power that lies in embracing the interconnectedness of all things. "In the dance of synthesis, seeker, harmonise the threads with an open spirit. Dance with fulfilment, for Cosmic Culmination unfolds when you allow the diverse elements to merge into a harmonious whole. Trust in the cosmic currents of

transformation, and let your dance be a unified waltz through the mysteries of existence."

Inspired by the World's words, the Fool posed another question, "Great Weaver, how does one attune themselves to the cosmic energies of fulfilment in the dance of synthesis? What wisdom guides the seeker in aligning with the transformative currents that flow through Cosmic Culmination?"

The World spoke of cosmic attunement, encouraging the Fool to become attuned to the energies of fulfilment and the dance of unity. "In the realm of synthesis, seeker, attune yourself to the cosmic energies. Feel the transformative currents that flow through Cosmic Culmination, and let your steps be in harmony with the unified dance of fulfilment. Align with the magic of unity, and become a conscious partner in the cosmic waltz of transformation."

As the conversation unfolded, the Fool felt a cosmic energy enveloping him. The realm, with its kaleidoscopic beauty and the World as a guide, became a transcendent landscape where the dance of synthesis revealed itself as a tapestry woven with threads of unity and fulfilment.

"Great Weaver, how does one invoke the magic of interconnectedness in the cosmic dance of synthesis? What wisdom guides the seeker in embracing the interwoven tapestry of existence and allowing unity to guide their steps through Cosmic Culmination?" the Fool inquired, aware of the profound interconnectedness often associated with the dance of synthesis.

The World acknowledged the intertwining dance of synthesis and interconnectedness, speaking of the importance of embracing the unity of all things. "In the cosmic dance of interconnectedness, seeker, embrace the interwoven threads. Allow synthesis to be a celebration of unity, for in Cosmic Culmination, the dance is enriched by your recognition of the interconnected tapestry of existence. Let unity guide your steps through the cosmic symphony."

Feeling the cosmic energies resonating within him, the Fool delved deeper into the conversation. "Great Weaver, how does one navigate the challenges of maintaining balance in the cosmic dance of synthesis? What wisdom guides the seeker in staying centred and finding equilibrium within Cosmic Culmination?"

The World spoke of the challenges inherent in the dance of synthesis, encouraging the Fool to maintain balance with centre redness. "In the realm of challenges, seeker, navigate the dance with a centred spirit. Maintain balance, for Cosmic Culmination unfolds when you stay attuned to the cosmic equilibrium and find stability within the transcendent mysteries. Face the challenges with the wisdom of the cosmic symphony."

As the transcendent conversation between the Fool and the World continued, the realm seemed to shimmer with a cosmic energy. The kaleidoscopic beauty, now a symbol of synthesis and fulfilment, became a vessel of cosmic unity where the dance unfolded with harmonious precision.

"Great Weaver, what role does gratitude play in the cosmic dance of synthesis? How does one foster introspection and find clarity in the reflection of their interconnected existence within Cosmic

Culmination?" the Fool inquired, sensing the profound connection between synthesis and the virtue of gratitude.

The World spoke of gratitude as the radiant glow in the dance of synthesis, urging the Fool to weave threads of introspection into the cosmic tapestry. "In the realm of reflection, seeker, let gratitude be the enchanting glow that bathes you in the cosmic symphony. Foster clarity in the reflection of your interconnected existence, and let the dance of Cosmic Culmination be a testament to the magic of appreciating the unity of all things. Through gratitude, you shall contribute to the harmonious symphony of cosmic transformation."

Expressing his gratitude, the Fool said, "Great Weaver, your wisdom has brought a sense of cosmic wonder to my journey. I carry the echoes of your teachings as I continue to dance through the realms of the grand tapestry. May Cosmic Culmination guide my steps."

The World, her presence encompassing the entirety of creation, nodded in acknowledgment. "May the cosmic dance unfold with the magic of synthesis's transcendent symphony. Go forth, seeker, and let Cosmic Culmination carry you to realms yet unveiled."

Leaving the realm of Cosmic Culmination, the Fool felt the cosmic energy lingering in his every step. The dance of synthesis whispered tales of unity and fulfilment, and the kaleidoscopic beauty accompanied him toward the next archway. The rhythmic dance of the cosmic tapestry echoed in his heart, and the World's transcendent teachings illuminated his path as he ventured into the uncharted territories that awaited in the chapters yet to unfold.

And thus, the Fool continued his journey, now a seasoned dancer in the cosmic tapestry, each step resonating with the echoes of the realms he had traversed. As he approached the next archway, the culmination of his odyssey unfolded—a journey that transcended the boundaries of time and space, weaving a tapestry of wisdom and transformation. The Fool embraced the unknown with open arms, for the dance of the cosmic tapestry was an eternal symphony, and he, the eternal dancer.

The Fool's journey, enriched with experiences that spanned exploration, transformation, balance, abundance, confrontation of temptation, embracing change, finding hope, navigating intuition and illusion, basking in joy, and self-reflection, continued its ascent toward its grand finale.

At the cosmic junction of Judgement's revelations, the Fool found himself on the cusp of the World—a realm where the celestial energies converged in a tapestry of transcendent magic. The cosmic symphony continued its enchanting melody as the Fool approached the apex of his mystical journey.

And here the landscape shifted one last time, leading the Fool to a place And here the landscape shifted one last time, leading the Fool to a place that felt like the culmination of his profound adventure. The air was charged with anticipation, and the surroundings seemed to resonate with the echoes of the past and the promise of the future.

The World unfolded before the Fool as a celestial mandala, intricately woven with symbols of cosmic wisdom and arcane symbolism. Each corner represented an elemental force, a guardian spirit, and a portal to realms beyond mortal comprehension. The Fool stepped into this sacred space, sensing the timeless embrace of past, present, and future converging in a cosmic dance.

As he ventured further into this culminating landscape, the Fool found himself standing before a colossal wreath, encircling a radiant woman who danced at the centre of it all. She was the World, a symbol of completion, integration, and the realization of one's purpose. The World's presence was awe-inspiring, and it embodied the essence of the entire journey, bringing together all the themes and teachings the Fool had encountered.

The World danced with grace and vitality, and her movements were a celebration of the unity and harmony that the Fool had sought throughout his remarkable journey. She began to speak with a voice that resonated like a beautiful symphony.

She explained that the journey had been a profound odyssey, not just about the individual themes, but about understanding that life was a tapestry of experiences, each interconnected and contributing to the wholeness of one's existence.

As she spoke Celestial energies whispered tales of completion and unity, and mythical beings, emissaries of cosmic realms, encircled the Fool. The convergence of elemental forces and mystical guardians marked not just an end but a cosmic rebirth—a fusion of cycles and the initiation of a new era in the eternal dance of existence.

In this magical tapestry, the Fool felt a profound sense of interconnectedness with the cosmic whole. The World's enchantment beckoned the Fool to transcend the boundaries of individuality, merging with the universal currents that wove through the threads of destiny.

The Fool, now a conduit of cosmic energies, became a co-creator in the ongoing symphony of creation.

As the Fool embraced the energies of cosmic unity, he realised that the journey had been a mystical pilgrimage—an odyssey of self-discovery and an exploration of the divine dance of life. The World's magic encouraged the Fool to celebrate not only the victories but also the lessons, acknowledging each thread woven into the intricate tapestry of his soul.

In the cosmic embrace of the World, the Fool felt a resonant connection with the universe—a recognition that their existence was an essential note in the grand cosmic composition. The mythical beings, guardians of cosmic truths, guided the Fool to dance in harmony with the celestial currents, transcending the limitations of the material realm.

The World emphasised the importance of recognising that every step of the journey, every lesson, and every encounter had led the Fool to this moment of fulfilment. She taught him that the journey was not just about the external landscapes and personal growth but also about embracing the interconnectedness of all things, acknowledging the vast web of life, and realising one's place within it.

As the Fool listened to the World's words, he felt a profound sense of unity and fulfilment. He understood that the journey was not just about personal development but about recognising the intricate dance of life itself and his role within it.

With a heart overflowing with gratitude and awareness, the Fool prepared to step through the celestial portal of the World. The journey had completed its cosmic cycle, marked by the profound realisation that every step, challenge, and revelation had been a magical thread contributing to the masterpiece of his existence.

As the Fool crossed the threshold, the cosmic symphony reached its crescendo, and a new cycle of the eternal dance commenced, leaving the Fool forever attuned to the enchantment of the cosmos.

The World had become his final guide, leading him to the realisation that life was not just about the landscapes explored but about the profound journey within, a journey that led to the understanding that every step, every experience, and every encounter was an integral part of the grand design of existence.

With this profound realisation, the Fool embraced the World's dance, joining in the celebration of life's interconnectedness. As he did, he recognised that his adventure was not just about reaching a final destination but about acknowledging the beauty of the entire journey, from the Fool's humble beginnings to this glorious culmination. The Fool had become a part of the world, and the world a part of him.

And so, the Fool's journey came to its grand finale, not as an end, but as a new beginning. With the wisdom and unity he had gained, the Fool was ready to continue his adventure, embracing life's ever-unfolding tapestry with open arms and a heart full of gratitude.

With his ever faithful companion by his side the fool knew that this part of his journey had come to a conclusion he would need all he had learnt to move forth into the lower realms that await.

~ Twenty-Three ~

The last word.......

The final end of the Fool's journey, emerged as a celebration of interconnectedness and the beauty of existence, marking not just an end but a cosmic rebirth—an initiation of a new era in the eternal dance of existence. The Fool, having embarked on a remarkable journey through the realms of the major arcana Tarot, had come full circle, forever attuned to the enchantment of the cosmos.